A Stones Throw

C M Cardwell

 New Generation Publishing

Dedication

This is dedicated to the memory of the late Dick Cardwell, who planted the seed of an idea for this novel with the stories he told of how his ancestors came to Lancashire.

The author C M Cardwell was born in Stoke on Trent in 1944. In 1947 the family moved to Blackpool to open a boarding house. During the season they used outbuildings, a bed settee in the lounge and the pantry as bedrooms. At school anthologies and stories were published in the magazine, and an English prize was presented before leaving. In 1966 was married and had two children and later two grandchildren, made stories up for them, which were later published in the Lancashire Authors Association magazine. At the age of 50 gained a GCSE in English at night school. Had an article published in Yours magazine and story and poems in Seasiders Write in 2006, also in a competition for Wyre Borough Councils book Grist to the Mill, which was performed on stage at Thornton Little Theatre. Wrote plays, one in collaboration called `Sweet dreams are made of this` for Fylde Arts at Lytham Assembly rooms. A publication sponsored by Blackpool Council called Diversions with poems and stories distributed to all railway stations. A poem was sent to Her Majesty the Queen on her Diamond Jubilee, an acknowledgement was received from Buckingham Palace. Read stories and poems on the radio for the blind which went all round the country. This debut novel is the first in a trilogy.

Acknowledgments

I would like to thank John for his help about his family's history of farming. Thanks also to Charmian Coates for all her help and to Elle- Marie Hinchcliffe. I am a member of the Blackpool Writers Circle and also Lancashire Authors Association.

Prologue

Every story has to start somewhere.

This one begins by a Lancashire river at high winters flood in December 1745. The Jacobite rebels were retreating from Derby. Four Mc Cardell brothers joined them many of whom like themselves were forced into this now failed rebellion. The Laird's men took them, leaving two sisters and sick brother on their croft on the highlands of Skye, in restitution for the tax they could not pay. During the many battles they experienced the anguish and horror of war. Each sustained injuries, but their psychological scars would never heal. The stench of death lingered along with the cries of the injured and mutilated bodies of their comrades. These illiterate peasants quickly learnt how to kill or be killed. Ordered to retreat from Derby on December the 6th they and thousands of others, fled before the might of King George's army came to wreak a terrible vengeance on them. This story explains what happened to them in the next two years

Chapter 1 Thomas

"Thomas we can nay stay." Richard, urged his eldest brother, as the four of them sat exhausted on the banks of a Lancashire river, on a bitter December day in 1745. Horrified, to see their fellow Jacobites swim the icy waters of a high winter's tide, desperate to reach their homeland before the Redcoats slaughtered them.

Thomas ignored him, and continued searching the ground.

"Aye he's right." Roberts's voice trembled. "We'll freeze to death staying here."

Thomas assumed that his brothers knew why he looked for stones, as wave after wave of their comrades plunged into the swollen river. Hundreds, like themselves were forced into this now failed rebellion, though many willingly offered up their lives, believing that Charles Edward Stuart was the rightful King. He had promised to relieve the miserable oppression suffered by the Scottish people at the hands of King George's army.

A large group of rebels preferred to retreat through the villages and hamlets instead of the city roads they came by; this seemed a better option so the brothers joined them. At the crossroads two lanes led away from Scotland, while the other lay across the bridge that passed the Manor House which was guarded. Leaving the road, they scrambled down the river bank towards a bend which was out of sight. It was a cold desolate place where the naked trees afforded them little shelter from the fierce North West winds and the reeds by the riverbank whistled wildly.

They all suffered injuries, from the many battles they fought and their feet bled from the hard ground of the English countryside. Panic was widespread, as

7

everyone tried to escape the Redcoats, fearing they would wreak a terrible vengeance on them.

The brothers watched those who made it to the opposite bank collapse exhausted , while others screamed in terror, as their bodies were swept away in the angry torrent.

These, and many other horrendous sights they experienced, would haunt them forever.

Thomas knew they could not swim, and so devised a plan of escape. He had taken responsibility for them all, after his mother's death and his father's breakdown. For twelve years he made decisions for his six siblings, till the Laird's men violently forced them away from their croft, because they had no crops to pay the tax. Their sisters Jinni and Ellen secreted their ailing brother John away, before watching distraught, as they were dragged off to fight for someone they had never even heard of.

They soon discovered that they lived on an island called Skye, before crossing by boat to a land known as Scotland. Where they learned to kill or be killed and fought many bloody battles through the garrison cities, before continuing into a country called England. They fought through Carlisle and on into Lancashire, eventually arriving at Derby on December the 6th. There the clan leaders were falsely informed that an English army, vastly outnumbering them was heading in their direction. But Charles Edward Stuart or Bonnie Prince Charlie as he was known as wanted to continue on for the 126 miles to London to claim his crown. The leaders disagreed and ordered the Jacobite army to retreat, before the Redcoats arrived.

Thomas assumed that he was about the same age as the Pretender, but the gulf between them was enormous. The Prince was handsome and highly intelligent, while he was shabby and illiterate. He

8

understood about his perseverance only not from loyalty, because as a boy he was the backbone of his family, but only out of guilt.

Now in the turmoil of a rapidly retreating army by that river bank, Thomas decided to stop running and regain control once again. Stones had always played an important part in their lives marking the graves of their dead, or settling any disputes.

"What will we do, Thomas?" Young William asked.

After weighing up the options, he answered.

"Aye, we'll use these stones to see which way to go, so the Redcoats dinna find us."

"Nay, what good's that, we canna go forward or back?" Richard questioned.

"Aye but at yon crossroads, we'll go the way our stones fall, and hope yon Redcoats go through the cities." Thomas replied.

"Aye, but what will we do without yee, and about going home?" Robert enquired.

"Nay, I was only a wee laddie when I took over, and yee're all grown men, find work and we'll be fine. Back home we dinna have enough to eat, leave it for the three of them. We dinna ken the way home anyway." Thomas reminded them.

"Aye he's right; we've fought like men, dinna we? If we can do that, we can do anything." William agreed.

Each then chose a different stone handing it to Thomas, with the river on one side and the advancing army on the other, he threw them up high. Richard and Robert's fell to the east, while his and William's fell to the west. There, four brothers footsore, battle scarred, and weary of fighting, were sad and afraid to part. Their clothes stained from months of sleeping rough, hugged each other for the first and last time.

Thomas already regretted his decision, but it was their only option, and he warned.

"We must be away afore the Redcoats come."

"Aye laddies, we may meet again one day." William encouraged them all so different in build and natures

"Nay, we've nere been apart afore." Robert spoke poignantly.

"Aye, we'll cross yon bridge together and if we make it, we'll meet again." Richard said.

At the crossroads they raised their arms to each other, knowing that their paths led them into the land of the enemy. Richard and Robert had the difficult task of crossing the bridge without being seen, as they risked being shot by any guards there.

Meanwhile Thomas questioned William, as they walked. "Why's life so hard?"

"Aye it was when leaving them on Skye, and now leaving Richard and Robert."

"Nay, I thought we'd be better alone, dinna ken if I'm right?" Thomas questioned.

"We'd nay have survived in those highlands without yee, and I'll nere forget all yee did for us." William consoled him.

Their conversation lapsed as they reached the road and William's words left a lump in his throat yet he managed to say. "Take care wee brave brother; I've always been proud on yee."

He embraced him again for a final time before they parted.

Thomas turned away quickly, and taking a deep breath set off down the lanes that lay ahead, constantly looking over his shoulder for the English army. He now carried another guilt, that his brothers had taken his advice, and these thoughts also lingered.

He kept close to the hedgerows shielding himself from the icy winds, as bitter as those on Skye; there was sparse shelter there too. Dormant frozen fields stretched out on each side, as leafless trees waved their skeletal branches in a wild menacing way. This land wore its winter clothes, cold and unfriendly, making him shiver. He pulled his tattered plaid around him for comfort, passing signposts he could not read.

He knew that daylight hours were short at this time of year, and he must find shelter or freeze to death. His stomach groaned, and to make things worse it began to snow. His thoughts returned to those back home, and he wondered if they were knee deep in snow. He recalled carrying heavy stones from the hills, to build a shelter for the goats and their hay, with enough peat for the fire in winter. He and Richard had cleared a path from the croft, so the goats milk could supplement their meagre diet. He hoped that Jinni and Ellen had done it this year, as John's chest was always bad in winter.

As he continued he noticed a cluster of farmhouses, it would have been grand if they had neighbours back home when they needed them, he mused. He passed many more that shone a welcoming light, but he remained outside chilled to the bone. Fearing to ask a stranger for work dressed as a marauding rebel with flaming red hair and bushy beard; they might think he'd slit their throats, even though he was unarmed.

Thomas heard the rumble of a cart and petrified it was the Redcoats, he hid under a hedge. His heart beat frantically the nearer it got, anticipating being slain where he hid. Were his brothers safe? He would never know, as the cart was almost upon him. Was he to die here hiding like a coward, after all he had gone through? As it approached a wheel hit a pot hole, sending it in his direction. Moving quickly away, he saw that it was only a farmer who was thrown out, and several empty milk churns were rolling in the snow. As it fell heavier, he saw the cart on its side, with a

11

terrified horse attached. His natural instincts took over, and he ran to calm the frightened animal just as the farmer got up, he was unsure if he might inform on him and nervously asked. "Are yee all right?"

"No bones broken, head must be made of wood." The man replied, tapping his forehead before dusting himself down.

"Thanks for looking after Daisy, or she'd have panicked. Glad all those churns are empty, or milk would be everywhere." Scratching his head he looked at the wheel. "Blast! It couldn't have happened at a worse time in this damned weather."

Thomas felt sorry for him, but knowing he was in danger if the Redcoats found him, he still offered to help. "Do ye need a hand?"

"That'd be grand, lad."

The last time he was called that, he dug a grave for his mother who died in childbirth. His father so full of grief didn't see that his seven children were also grieving. He helped his brothers and sister to carry their bodies up the hill from the croft, burying them next to her two children who died earlier. His father had revealed a terrible secret to him in anger when his mother died, but afterwards never spoke again, leaving him and Richard to fill in the grave. The farmer's voice brought him back.

"Come on big lad, or we'll be knee deep in snow." It was only then, did he notice Thomas's kilt. "Here, aren't you a Jacobite?"

"Nay from choice."

"What do you mean?"

Thomas was afraid, but had to trust him and explained. "Aye we four brothers were taken from our croft on Skye, because we dinna pay the Laird's tax. At Derby they sent us back, and at the river we canna

12

swim, so we threw stones up like we did back home, and went the way they fell."

"My God lad, that's bad."

Thomas nodded, and then easily lifted up the cart, while the farmer replaced the wheel, later they retrieved the churns and the man thanked him.

"I'm Harry Hodkin, but they call me Harry Hock, what's your name?"

"Thomas Mc Cardell." He answered nervously

"Well, Tom Cardell, I need a strong man on my farm, how about it?" Harry said.

"Aye please." He replied eagerly, accepting his callused hand by way of agreement, relieved not to spend the night outdoors.

Harry was in his mid forties with a weathered complexion and grey eyes that sparkled mischievously. His moleskin britches and snuff coloured shirt were well worn, the dark jacket was tied with twine, and his black shoes and beret had seen better days.

They had not travelled far, when Harry suggested.

"You'd best lose that skirt and your beards a mite scary, before the Redcoats see it."

"Aye, scary or nay, it kept my face warm on yon highlands." He never said it also covered a scar that he received in one of the battles they fought.

"You can wear some of my clothes, so folks don't know who you are, not that I mind."

"Aye but Harry yee dinna ken me."

"You've a good heart, Tom, and that's enough for me. We'll say you're my nephew from up north at Eastrick, that's come to help."

"Aye, but what be their name?" He enquired, with a frown.

"Bessie's my sister and Ted's her husband."

"Nay, what if I forget?"

It had all happened so fast, one minute he was hiding for his life, and the next he's called something else. This was yet another secret he had to keep.

"Folks aren't interested in my family, Tom, so don't worry."

But worry he did.

They drove on until Harry turned onto a cinder path with hedges on each side, leading into a cobbled yard. To his left there was an impressive farmhouse, and along the yard was a huge barn. Opposite was another building, which he later discovered housed the cattle in winter. Pulling up by a stable that could also fit the cart in, he jumped down barking his orders.

"Get in that barn, I'll bring some watter and clothes, so you can get rid of that thing off your face and that skirt, before meeting the wife and daughter."

Thomas entered the barn and could not believe his eyes. It was stacked high with sheaves of hay and straw, and in a storeroom next to it were countless sacks of grain. It would have fed them all year back home, even paying the Laird's tax, and then they might never have had to leave. He was still upset that Harry had called his beard a thing and his kilt a skirt, but knew he had to change to be accepted. Harry returned with hot water, shaving tackle and some clothes, taking his kilt to dispose of it.

After washing, Thomas shaved and in doing so opened up the scar on his face from a Redcoat's bayonet, later he bathed his cold and tender feet. Harry's clothes were tight on his muscular frame, so he left the thick soled shoes unfastened. The britches were rough but warm and dry and they smelt funny. Thomas no longer looked like a Jacobite, but a twenty four year old man, as he headed towards the farmhouse.

At the door, he was confronted by a pretty young woman, on her way out. Her fair curly hair and healthy

14

complexion enhanced her cornflower blue eyes, taking his breath away. Thomas only knew his sisters, but she captivated him.

"Hello! You must be Cousin Tom? I'm Alice, pleased to meet you."

She held out her slender hand, and he nervously shook it. Wishing he still had a beard to hide his blushes and the bleeding scar on his face, and he hoped his long hair covered it.

"Aye it's grand to meet yee too Alice lassie." He replied.

"Does Aunty Bessie and Uncle Ted speak like that? Mind you Dad and Mum speak normal like me." She remarked

Thomas had acquired a smattering of English, and tried hard to hide his Scottish brogue.

"I'm off to tend Daisy, go inside Mum's dying to meet you."

She pulled her red cape over a pretty blue striped dress and white pinny and ran across the snowy yard in her black leather shoes to the stable. She reminded him of his younger sister Ellen, only her hair was red like his. Thomas could imagine her huddled by the fire in the croft; he recalled how she cried when we were taken away and like Jinni and John, never knowing if they would ever see us again. He wished he could tell them they were all safe, or were the last time he saw them, but the guilt of lying to Harry's family only added to all the others. His heart was heavy as he opened the door, where he was greeted by a good smell of cooking, and a roaring fire, this room was bigger than their croft.

"Come in, Tom, you must be frozen through and starving to death, coming so far, get something warm inside you?" Harry's wife fussed.

Thomas feared Harry had told her everything, until she mentioned.

"Never been out of Lancashire myself, let alone Eastrick."

He was relieved, only did not know her name. "Aye thank yee Aunty?"

"Maggie will do, does Harry's sister and husband talk strange like that? Lucky you were there to help, or goodness knows how he would have managed alone in this weather? Is your face bleeding Tom?"

"It'll have been when he saw to Daisy, Maggie? And how do we know how they speak up there, anyhow." Harry blurted out and she nodded.

"I'll get something for it." She returned, with a clean rag handing it to him.

"Thank yee Maggie." He replied, relieved Harry had made an excuse about his brogue.

Later, she handed him a hot meat and potato pie out of the oven from inside the black grate by the fire. Her sleeves were rolled up on her green floral dress revealing the dimpled elbows of her bulky frame. Wiping her brow, with the white apron that matched her mobcap, she talked constantly as he devoured his meal.

"Blackmoor Moss, is agricultural and livestock land, I was born here and my parents before me. I met Harry when he was helping Sam at Cunningham mill, as Annie almost lost her baby. He and your mother worked on a farm close by and were orphans, but you'll know that. I never met her, as she and your father had moved away. I told Father that Harry was the one, and he gave him a job, the rests history, and we ran the farm after they died."

Tom nodded and understood why Harry never spoke much.

"You're in time for Christmas Tom, we have a good time here, don't we, Harry?"

"We do Maggie, but Tom needs new clothes by then, he spoilt his fixing the wheel." Harry winked.

But it did not ease his mind.

"Show Tom to his room, he looks dead beat poor soul, while I wash up."

Thomas now Tom, was glad to go, and as they left the table Alice returned.

"Have you met Tom, lass?"

"Yes Dad, we met as I went to tend Daisy." She replied shaking the snow off her cape.

Tom followed Harry upstairs, a first for him as their croft was on one level, and he showed him into a room. There stood a double bed with a feather throw on it, a chest of drawers on one wall and a chair by the window, overlooking the snowy fields.

Tom, though amazed, sat on the bed and explained his worries.

"Aye, Harry yee've been grand giving me a job, but I canna stay."

"Why ever not?" Harry gasped.

"Nay I canna get new clothes for this Christmas thing, Maggie's on about."

Harry laughed, realising that he had not explained anything to Tom.

"Listen lad, I`m not just offering you shelter from them that's after you, not lightly. I need help, and you're the man for it. You'll get paid, so you can buy clothes that fit. Now about this Christmas, it's a time of good will to all men when a baby came to save the world. We share gifts, and have friends round to remember him, it's time you enjoyed yourself, what do you say?"

"What did a bairn, save the world from?"

"From all our sins, of course."

"Nay, what's a sin?"

"Killing, stealing, or other bad things."

"Aye, then I'm a sinner, will he save me?"

"You were forced to."

"I ken that, but I still dinna ken anything about getting paid?"

"I'll teach you, so is it a deal then?"

"Aye it's a deal, and I'll work hard for yee, Harry."

They shook hands again to seal it, and Tom was glad to be there. Harry left him to get some much needed sleep in his own bed and room, his first ever. The stone he threw by the river, he placed on the drawers, it had indeed been lucky for him. He hoped that his brothers were safe, and not killed by the Redcoats. Exhausted, he slept soundly till the morning, and awoke unsure if it had been a dream. Till the smell of bacon and eggs wafted up the stairs, and he knew then it was true, after all the things he had endured.

Christmas soon came; it was a mixture of trauma, celebrations, and meeting strangers. Lads who helped at harvest time made eyes at Alice, and strangely it upset him. It was the first time he had tasted Harry's Elderberry wine, and it certainly had quite a kick.

*   *   *

Over the next six months, Tom's beard covered his scar but he never left the farm.

"Come to the mill today, I could do with some company?" Harry pleaded yet again.

"Nay I canna there's cows to milk, and the granary to clear, afore the harvest."

As they talked, Maggie brought out Harry's bagging, to eat on the journey.

"Don't forget my sack of flour, or that dried fruit from the market?"

Harry bent over to take it, and then yelled out in pain as his back locked.

Maggie screamed, making Tom run from the barn, and he carefully lifted Harry down, and carried him into the house. Maggie left the door open, and sent Alice up for bedclothes, to prepare a makeshift bed on the settle. He gently lay the injured and ever complaining Harry down.

"Be careful, my back's broken, now you'll have to go, Tom, won't you?"

"Nay I dinna ken the way?" He gasped.

"Our Alice does, she'll show you?" Harry replied.

"I can't Dad, I'm washing the clothes?" She explained.

"Leave it lass, I'll do it when I've settled your father down, now hurry up, and don't forget what I wanted, Tom." Maggie interjected.

He nodded, and in a fluster grabbed his jacket from a nail behind the door, pleased only to be going with Alice.

She removed her wet pinafore, and putting on her bonnet, yelled.

"Come on then Tom, now let's be off?"

Chapter 2 William

William doubted his own bravery and felt undeserving of Thomas's pride. He missed his brothers but was glad they all survived the rebellion. His own side had been pierced by a Redcoat's bayonet, and his feet bled. These scars could heal but the memories would remain. He was determined to succeed in this new life, which might even be an adventure. In time he reached a town where wagons and carts carried livestock to an auction. Each farmer that passed threw strange glances his way, he knew then it would be hard finding work dressed as a rebel. His idea about it being an adventure rapidly faded. He feared that Redcoats were about, so he sensibly took the back lanes.

Resting by a pebbled wall, he watched as three elderly ladies struggled to get two calves out of a cart. Realising he was in danger by offering he enquired.

"Canna I help yee?"

The eldest, a stiff backed, lady whose grey hair showed beneath a white bonnet, had flinty eyes that glared at him, her severe thin lips and wrinkled face made him nervous. She wore a long black dress with a white lacy collar and pinafore, as her scraggy hands twisted in annoyance trying to ignore him. The younger lady's face was more pleasant with steel blue eyes and her mousy hair was plaited round her head. She too was slim and dressed like the older woman but in grey and she pleaded with her.

"We can't do it, so let him try?"

A third lady was bigger built with a jolly face and deep blue eyes that sparkled. Her dark hair was also plaited and was dressed like the others but in navy as she steadied the horse.

The eldest relented. "Do what you want; I don't trust any man, especially one in a skirt!"

A jovial voice came from the front of the cart.

"And how many men have you seen, wearing a skirt?"

The humourless old woman sniffed, before storming into the cottage.

William had never seen such a place; it had a thatched roof and whitewashed walls, while pretty curtains hung from dainty windows. The front garden was surrounded by a low pebbled wall, just like the one he rested by. He thought how different it was from their croft which was called a blackhouse, because the smoke from the peat fire could only escape through gaps in the door or window. It was only as big as the building next to the cottage, where he assumed the calves were going. He recalled how nine of them huddled together from the highland winds and it didn't seem fair.

He jumped onto the cart and with a twinge of pain, asked.

"Aye and where are they away to?"

The youngest pointed to a field opposite.

"Canna they go over yonder?" He enquired.

"The outhouse indeed, is only for storing things in." The bigger lady explained, tittering.

What a waste he mused, facing a bleak night under a hedge until he found work. As he struggled with the calves, sweat dripped off his auburn hair revealing its natural kink, before falling onto his silky beard.

"Aye have yee rope to tie one so yon other will follow?"

The youngest ran to the outhouse and returned with it. "Will this do?"

"Aye thanks Miss." He replied, while tying it round a calf's neck.

"I'm Martha, this is Ruth and our sister is Agnes, what's your name?"

"William Mc Cardell, dinna anyone help yee with jobs like this?"

"Agnes doesn't trust men, not since she was jilted, so we have to manage. We did get the old cow on for slaughter, we only needed one calf, but they're twins so we took both."

He understood and also why Agnes was so nasty, as he manoeuvred the first calf out.

"Aye stand aside ladies, we're away out."

Ruth watched the other while Martha closed the gate.

They put them in the calving pen near to where cows sheltered under a wooden shed.

"I hope we've not kept you from your work, William?" Ruth enquired.

"I've nay job yet; yee dinna ken where I can get one?"

"Wait here? It's strange but Father was called William." Martha smiled.

They scurried into the cottage, and as he wiped the sweat from his brow, it began to snow. He shivered and hoped that he could survive this storm without shelter, though back home he was used to the cold, but they slept indoors with a peat fire to warm them.

Agnes then led her sisters out, speaking sharply to him.

"Mr Mc Cardell, I believe that's your name?"

"Aye it is."

"My sisters tell me that you are seeking work?" She continued

"Aye, I am."

"It's against my better judgement, but if you work here, the job's yours." She snapped.

"Thank yee, but I dinna have anywhere to stay."

"Use the outhouse, only with food the wage is less, what do you say?"

He thought her abruptness verged on rudeness, but it beat the hedge any day.

"Aye, thanks Agnes."

Her eyes almost popped out of her head, before she turned in disgust back into the cottage. Ruth and Martha beamed and showed him to his new home. On entering his heart sank, it was filled with every conceivable working implement, boxes, and trunks all covered in dust and cobwebs. A bed by one wall was laden with rope and twine, and a window that was filthy.

"I know it's a mess, but we can make it better." Martha admitted.

"Let's clear a space, so you can sleep here tonight." Ruth suggested.

They stacked everything in a corner, but left out a large trunk. Martha cleaned the window making it lighter, and seeing his wet clothes she suggested.

This was Father's trunk you can use anything out of it?" Martha said.

"We'll make you comfortable." Ruth added.

They left him to sit exhausted on the bed, glad to be indoors and to rest his side.

Martha returned with a bowl of hot water and a towel, Ruth followed armed with covers for his bed before leaving him again to get cleaned up. He'd never been the centre of attention before and now he'd never be called wee William ever again.

He used items from the trunk, shaved and cut his straggly soaked hair. His face now naked, he bathed his injured side and bleeding feet. Old William's clothes smelt musty and the black britches felt strange as he was used to bare legs. The handmade grey shirt and black jacket fitted him perfectly as he gingerly put on the knitted socks and black leather shoes. He hid his bloodstained kilt in the trunk so the ladies would not find it.

Later, Ruth brought in bread, cheese and hot milk and gasped.

"My! You are handsome."

Martha followed carrying a homemade apple pie and also gasped.

"Goodness me, you look so different."

"Aye, thank yee ladies, that food smells grand."

They smiled and left him, unaware that he was practically starving. They returned later with more bedding and he felt that Ruth fussed over him like a mother hen over her chick, but he liked it.

"Nay I hope Agnes is nay still mad at yee?"

"She'll be fine when she knows all men aren't like Henry Brady." Ruth explained.

"You're in time for Christmas, we're having goose for dinner, and its ten years since a man ate with us." Martha delighted in saying.

"Nay is that when yon father died?"

The smiles left their faces, so he changed the subject.

"Aye tell me what yon Christmas is?"

"Aren't you a Christian, William?" They chimed together.

"Nay, on Skye, we seven bairns dinna ken anyone after our parents died. The first ones we met forced four of us to be Jacobites."

They sat down heavily on the trunk, and Martha explained.

"We thought it was bad running the farm after Father died."

"When Agnes was to marry we hoped things would change, but it didn't, so now we'll all die as Bradmans." Ruth added.

24

"Dinna say that, tell me about Christmas?"

"A long time ago a baby was born who was the son of God." Ruth began.

"Aye is God like the Laird?"

"He's greater than whoever the Laird is, or even King George." Martha responded.

"On his birthday, we give small gifts to remember him." Ruth added.

"We've nere heard of this and I've nay gifts."

"You can buy things when you get paid, and we'll all go to Freestone." Ruth explained. "But you should sleep now, you look exhausted." Martha added.

After they left William was too tired to worry about any of that, but looked through the window at the snow covered garden behind the cottage. He noticed a shed and wondered what it was for. The snow was bad here but not as deep as on Skye, and he hoped his brothers were not out on this cold night, or if they were all safe.

This was his first experience of a Christmas and also joining the Bradmans going to church. Agnes never changed her attitude even when the Reverend talked about the joy of the Saviour's birth. This confirmed everything that the two sisters had already told him. But most of all he enjoyed hearing Ruth and Martha singing their hearts out to carols that he had never heard before. One particular carol had made complete sense to him, though he had no idea where the place was that they mentioned.

Long time ago in Palestine
Upon a wintry mourn
All in a lowly cattle shed
The Prince of Peace was born

He was a friend of all the poor
That wanders here below;
It was His only joy on earth
To ease them of their woe.

(A Christmas Carol, by Edwin Waugh, from poems and songs of old Lancashire.)

It seemed to him that this Prince cared more for people like him and his brothers, than the Prince they fought for, he thought. Returning home later they exchanged gifts before dinner, and the goose was the finest meal he had ever tasted. Agnes spoilt it though by remaining aloof; but Ruth and Martha were always kind.

*   *   *

William stayed and tolerated Agnes and her ways, but she always found work for him. He milked the cows and Martha weaned the calves while Ruth collected eggs from the chickens in shed in the back garden. Agnes ran the home and business, paying the bills with the money they made. He and Martha took their produce in the cart before driving it along the shore line, which was at the end of the lane but only when the tide was out, to Lymouth where they sold them.

"I can nay do money Martha? But Ruth told me that when the fruit in the orchard ripens we'll sell that too."

She nodded and enjoyed his company.

Later on he repaired the cowshed, his confidence boosted he fixed the thatched roof. His brothers did it on their croft when the straw rotted from the smoke off the fire. Ruth and Martha made work clothes for him, so he saved old William's for Sunday's. But it was Reverend Parker's daughter Emily who took his eye as she always smiled at him.

Things changed when Agnes contracted a bad chest like his brother John, she missed the services and the Reverend and Emily were worried about her. William was replacing cobbles in the garden wall on a bright spring day. He dwelt on how heavy they were and was glad that the stones they threw by the river that day weren't as big, or they would not have lived to tell the story. He was so absorbed and totally unaware of being watched.

"It is a lovely day for working outside, William?"

Looking serene in a brown fitted dress, her dark hair tucked neatly under her crisp white bonnet, and her ebony eyes smiling at him, was Emily.

"Nay I dinna see yee there Emily, have yee come to see Agnes?"

"Yes, and I've some books for her, how is she today?"

"Nay change, but she'd love to see yee."

Wiping his hands on his work clothes, he opened the gate for her and shouted upstairs. "Emily's here to see Agnes."

"Ask her to come in William, she'll cheer her up." Ruth replied.

She smiled while passing him and he breathed in her feminine essence.

"Nay, I'm dirty, Emily lassie."

"You must never be ashamed about doing honest toil, William."

As the door closed his heart raced, hoping that he might stand a chance with her. He quickly finished and rushed to wash and change before she left.

Her eyes lit up seeing him look so smart.

"So you have finished, William and what a fine job you have done. Agnes said you were a Godsend and does not know how they ever managed without you."

She smiled and her mesmerising eyes stirred his heart.

"Aye, did she? Err... Emily canna I walk yee home?"

"Thank you William, I will enjoy your company on this lovely sunny day."

He would have offered whatever the weather.

"How long have you been a member of the Church, William?" She enquired.

"Nay I dinna."

"What do you mean?"

He was afraid to say at first, but then explained.

"Aye our parents died when I was only a wee laddie and we seven bairns stayed in our croft on Skye. Thomas and Jinni were our parents and they were only bairns too. John was nay well and he looked after me and Ellen. Last year some men came and made four of us go to fight in the Jacobite army." He explained everything and added. "Aye and at the river Thomas threw our stones up like we always did, and mine sent me here."

"Where did the others go?"

"Nay we canna read, so I dinna ken."

There was a prolonged silence, making him worry.

"If you do want to read William, I have the books to teach you."

"Nay me read! Dinna the Reverend mind?"

"Father will be pleased so that you can follow the services, do come after work."

28

"Aye I will!" He beamed, but was unaware that all the books were from the Bible.

"Thank you for walking me home William, we can start tomorrow, goodbye till then?" "Aye I'll be there, goodbye, Emily lassie."

They spent every evening together for the next two months, she was as eager to teach as he was to learn, and even Reverend Parker encouraged it.

While William's life improved, Agnes's deteriorated. He was about to leave as usual, when Ruth called him back.

"William! Get the doctor, it's Agnes!"

He ran to get him and soon returned in his carriage, and he waited with Ruth and Martha.

As he descended the stairs, his face was sombre.

"I'm sorry but there is nothing more I can do, you must send for her minister."

Ruth and Martha were distraught and William hated to leave them, but volunteered.

"Aye I'll go, but will yee two be all right?"

"I'll stay with the ladies, till you return." The doctor informed him.

After thanking him, he ran and banged on the vicarage door. Emily was stunned as she opened it

"Nay, it's Agnes; the Reverend's to come afore she dies!" He blurted.

"Please get the buggy ready William, and we can all go?" She asked in a fluster.

It was ready for a pale faced vicar and an anxious looking Emily to get aboard. William drove at full gallop, stopping only to let the Reverend dash upstairs, and the doctor left. He and Emily remained with Ruth and Martha, the atmosphere was morose as they waited for Reverend Parker to come down with the inevitable news.

"Agnes died peacefully in my presence, do accept my deepest sympathy."

"But we never said goodbye!" Ruth broke down.

"What will we do without her?" Martha cried out.

He remembered Robert saying that; and though William felt their pain, Agnes had lived longer than his parents. Being the man of the house he thanked the vicar.

"Aye Agnes would be glad yee were there Reverend, but what happens now?"

"She'll be buried in the family plot in the churchyard, won't she?"

"Certainly Ruth, but the doctor must sign the death certificate first." The Reverend said. "Aye I'll fetch him and dig the grave, if yee like?" William offered.

"Yes please William, but the gravediggers will do that!" Ruth explained.

"May we take the buggy Father, it will be quicker?" Emily asked

"Yes do, I will console the ladies."

They left before hearing any response, and on the way Emily touched his hand as he held the reins, and it felt right somehow.

"Agnes would be pleased by your kind offer, William."

Two days later he took Agnes in a plain wooden coffin on her final journey, in their Sunday carriage. Emily followed in the Reverend's buggy with Ruth and Martha. It was very different from his parents' simple burials under the tree behind the croft and marked with stones. After the service and internment, he took Ruth and Martha home, before returning to fill in the grave. Jinni had told him that Thomas and Richard did it for their mother, as their father's mind and heart was broken. He knew that Agnes was a difficult woman to love, no wonder Henry Brady changed his mind.

Later, he brightened looking forward to another lesson with Emily. His reading was doing well, as was their relationship which blossomed daily. It was arranged that he be accepted into the Church of England on his 19th birthday May 5th. After discussing it with everyone he dropped the Mc from his name to become simply William Cardell. He wondered what his brothers would think about it. Ruth and Martha were his sponsors and it was only on this occasion that Reverend Parker realise how his and Emily's relationship had developed. The Reverend's mind had been preoccupied of late to notice it. The Squire, who is the patron of the church, brought unsettling potentially life-changing news.

William and Emily's future looked bright, and for the first time in his life he was happy. But judging from all his past experiences, he should have known that nothing should ever be taken for granted.

Chapter 3 Richard

Richard reassured Robert that they could cross the bridge safely, even though their comrades swam the dangerous river, rather than risk being slaughtered by guards at the Manor House opposite. While they deliberated, fate dealt them a helping hand in the form of farmer's slow moving cart laden with milk churns. Hurriedly, they scrambled aboard and hid between them. For a heart stopping moment it slowed down at the Manor House, petrified they huddled together afraid of being caught. The cart stopped at the side gate and they braced themselves for what might happen. While it waited, they vacated their sanctuary taking shelter under a bush until the coast was clear.

They watched as the farmer entered and he remained oblivious of the illicit cargo he had unwittingly carried. The brothers waited until then before heading to another crossroads where they separated. Raising his hand to Robert was a defining moment in his life, but he was afraid that his timid brother would not be able to cope alone. It would be hard enough for him; in the security of his family he was confident, but now even he doubted himself. Reluctantly, he threw his stone by the river; and now like his brothers he faced an unknown future. He walked for miles with difficulty, due to an injured knee caused by a shot from a Redcoat's musket. At a fork in the road he chose which path to take, and farmers working the land appeared wary of him. This land looked more fertile than the scrubland they tried to grow crops on back home. He continued on until reaching the brow of a hill, where in the valley below stood a windmill in all its glory. Four enormous black sails contrasted against the white walls, and a huge waterwheel was driven by a stream running beside it.

"Aye what a place to live." He muttered aloud.

A single cart remained and the man had unloaded his last sack. The cart that left earlier passed by and that farmer eyed him with suspicion, the other passed later and he completely ignored him. It made Richard more determined to see if the Miller was more amenable. The clouds began to gather and he knew the signs. As he neared, the Miller came down the steps dressed in white, and in desperation he spoke.

"Aye tis a fine mill yee have." He ignored the dark eyes that leered at him and persisted. "Do yee need a worker?"

The Miller removed the white cap, revealing long flowing raven hair which cascaded over her white smock.

"Nay I thought yee were yon Miller." He gulped.

"I am the Miller, for now." She replied, looking at him also with suspicion.

Stunning him momentarily, until he quickly regained his composure.

"Aye it mun be hard on yee own?"

"When Mother, died I helped Father but now that his chest is bad I'm doing it."

"I've nay worked in a mill afore, but I'm willing to learn?"

"You don't expect me, to risk our business to a scruffy man in a skirt, and let him ruin what my family have worked so hard for?"

"Aye well do it lassie, Miss high and mighty." He lashed out and turned to leave.

"Don't you call me lassie or Miss high and mighty; I'm a single woman who's not prepared to let a down and out like you take advantage of her."

"Nay looking like this dinna make me a down and out; I'm here through nay fault of my own." His face flushed, as he spit out the last line and it shocked her.

"Well, it might just be worth giving you a chance. Get in that stable over there and I'll bring water and proper clothes, then we'll think about it."

Richard was angry enough to refuse, but the first flakes of snow began to fall. It soaked his sandy hair and beard, so the thought of spending a night outside, made his decision easy. He waited till she brought in a pail of water, and threw some clothes at him.

"These are my father's shaving things and he'll decide if you can stay." She then left.

He washed and shaved his beard, then bathed his knee and bleeding feet. The clothes were too big even for Thomas, he thought. "Nay what ere ails yon miller, he's nay starving to death." He muttered again, pulling the belt tighter round his waist, before putting his sore feet into the large boots.

Richards face now exposed and his legs lost in the baggy white britches which fortunately did not rub his knee, he knocked on the door behind the mill. She opened it, having discarded her white smock, to reveal a voluptuous figure in a tight fitting bodice and matching yellow chintz skirt.

"Oh! You, look almost normal."

"Aye, Miss high and mighty, I am normal."

The smile changed the look on her face and made it quite attractive, he thought.

"Come in Father is waiting."

He entered cautiously, into a cosy room with a blazing fire and a table set for two, with three large comfy looking chairs. On the whitewashed walls were hand painted plates with views of the mill and the countryside around. A loud voice boomed out from one of the chairs and this man's build was no surprise to him.

"Come here...let's have...a look...at you."

He stood in front of a round faced bald headed older man. His head shone from the flames off the fire, and the heat made his face sweat. His sunken dark eyes glared at him, just as his daughter's had, only her hair and good looks must have come from her mother, he assumed.

"My daughter... Molly... says ... you're a... wronged... man?"

This old man, struggled hard to breathe, he thought.

"Aye, I'm Richard Mc Cardell, thank yee for yon clothes."

Molly sniggered at him, and he wanted to slap her.

"So... you were... forced... into this...rebellion?" The old man struggled.

Richard was aware he was in danger but defiantly stood his ground.

"Aye and my brothers."

"We're... taking a.... risk with ....you." The Miller continued unmoved.

Sorry as Richard was for the man, this annoyed him.

"Nay I'm taking a risk, with my life." Richard replied angrily.

The old man nodded.

"You've ...not... worked ... in a ...mill...?"

"Nay." He replied abruptly.

"At least...you're...honest." The Miller retorted

"Aye at most I'm honest, and a good worker!" He answered indignantly.

The man coughed at his audacity, so much that his face reddened. Molly's concern for him shone through.

"Have some water, Dad."

"Don't...fuss...it's...the...Millers...curse...flour...in ...the...lungs. mills...are...dangerous ...places...to work...will you...risk it...boy?"

"Aye, I'll try, and hope my lungs hold out, but how dangerous is yon mill?" Richard asked, angry at being called a boy; he was a brave warrior of twenty two.

"Father means that when the flour is ground it gets very hot and can explode; some Millers have been killed when the grinding stones broke up." Molly explained.

"Nay, why dinna it happen here?" Richard questioned.

"Our stones... are dressed... often... so it... won't...happen." The old man replied.

"If you're scared, then you'd best go now." Molly goaded.

"Nay if a wee lassie can do it, so can I." He reacted.

"Molly... needs help...at...the... harvest... so... you'd ...best... stay."

"I only need help Dad, till you are better."

She showed her disapproval by taking her anger out on Richard.

"Come on then Dick! I'll show you where you can sleep." Richard was bemused.

"You're Dick, and just Cardell, we don't want folks knowing who you are."

She led the way upstairs and he limped up after her, not mentioning he had never seen stairs before. Here it was clean and light, not dark like their croft; he entered a room which had a single bed, a small a set of drawers, and a chair. Molly began to explain.

"This mill at Cunningham has been in the Hargreaves family for generations, and I'm the last. I've to be sure you'll stay, and not just leave if something better comes along?"

"Aye I'll stay, yee are lucky living here, and I ken that when I first saw it." He admitted.

The smile of relief lit up her eyes, and for a moment she appeared vulnerable, before quickly changing the subject.

"It's not much, but it's somewhere to sleep."

She was so close that he felt her breath on his neck; he could smell the scent of spring flowers. Her soap wasn't like the Lye soap his mother made, and she intrigued him.

"Nay it's the first bed of my own; we five brothers slept in one corner of our croft, my two sisters in another and our parents at the far end. After they died, we older laddies slept in their room, and that's when Thomas, took over."

"I'd not know anything about that." She shrugged.

"Aye then yon lucky Molly, or is it Miss Hargreaves, or even Miss high and mighty?"

"Molly`s fine, tomorrow we'll get some whites that fit you."

Richard's anxiety showed.

"What's wrong, nobody knows who you are?"

"Nay, I'm used to hand me downs."

"I'm not surprised, but you've to dress right for the mill." She smirked.

"Aye and how do I get them?"

"I'll pay for the first set, and you pay for anything else you need."

"PAY! What with?" He visibly paled.

"You'll be paid for working, and you can use that."

"Nay this is all new to me?"

"Watch me tomorrow, I've to get things in for Christmas; I hope it cheers Father up?"

"Get things for what?"

"Don't you celebrate Christmas, where you come from?"

"Nay, we dinna cel e brate anything."

"What strange ways you people have."

"It's nay as strange as yee having a Christmas."

She smiled and briefly outlined what it was about and that presents were exchanged.

"Aye yee mun show me about that too?"

"I will, but come down now and we'll have something to eat."

Going down was easier and soon the table was filled with home made cakes and pastries. She saw to her father first and then they ate, but before they'd finished he moaned.

"I'm... ready ... for. ...bed...Molly!"

Though he was starving and could have eaten more, but taking the hint he bade them goodnight and she nodded to him. The exertion took its toll on the old man who coughed for hours before finally falling asleep. He heard Molly get into bed through the wall that divided them; and it sent shivers down his spine, a strange and new experience for him.

Dick looked out at the snow covered mill, knowing how fortunate he was, hoping his brothers were safe and not dead in a ditch somewhere. He was sad he could not tell them he was safe, if they lived Thomas and William would survive, but would Robert manage. It was his first Christmas and Molly tried hard to cheer her father up, but he was too ill.

*   *   *

Over the months, Molly taught him all about the mill.

"Keep clear of these millstones, and remember that the sails turn the top stone and the waterwheel turns the other."

"Aye, but how do yon sacks get down, do we use yon pulley we lift them up with?"

"We use this trapdoor here, they slide down a chute so the farmer can load them, and he pays us for doing it."

"What if he dinna need all of them?"

"We ask them as they load their sacks."

"Aye so what happens then?"

"I'll take the cost off and keep the sacks; we sell them to passing travellers or local villagers when they require them."

"Will yee teach me numbers, so I can help yee more?"

"If you're so eager I will, but you have trouble with your leg, will it be hard for you?"

"Nay it's an injury from the war; it only bothers me using the mill steps. I'd have died if Thomas hadna removed the shot with a dirk he found on yon battlefield and sealed it on an open fire."

"I'd no idea, will you be all right?"

"Aye I'll be grand, thank yee."

Molly was his boss in the mill and Sam was in the house, which often irked him. But it was a far cry from the ghastly sights he saw, and from which he still suffered nightmares.

Next day Molly informed him of some bad practices that happen.

"Some Millers put sand at the bottom of a sack, and still charge the full price for it. This gave us all a bad name; but we're honest and farmers come for miles to get a fair deal."

"Nay wonder yee are proud on it."

"I'll ask Jack Parkinson, to dress the stones when he comes."

"Does he always, do it?"

"Father used to but he can't now, Jack's a grinder anyway."

"Aye and what else does he grind?"

"Mostly metal such as scythes, blades and knives, but he'll do it for us."

"Aye I'd like to see that."

"You will, I'll show you how to put the brake on the wheel and sails, so he'll be safe. But we've done enough for now, let's have some dinner?"

Old Sam's appetite and weight had deteriorated; he coughed as bad as his brother John. Dick feared that he would not survive the summer, though his mind was still alert.

"Ask Parkinson...to dress...stones...and get ... Dick... to check... his ...metal?"

"I've told him Dad, don't fret."

Dick looked amazed, but she shook her head.

On returning to the mill, she explained.

"A true grinder has bits of metal on his arms from the sparks off the blades, and that's what show him your metal means."

"Aye, it sounds bad." He grimaced.

He looked at the grinding stones, and knew how stones always played a part in his life.

The view from up in the mill amazed him; he saw hills way in the distance. The fields had been ploughed and the seeds were shooting up and far off cows and sheep grazed. It was different from their little croft and he wondered if Jinni and Ellen were managing, he hoped John was well enough to help if their weather was good as it was here.

It was May and the blossoms were out on the hawthorn bushes, when the grinder came. Molly brought him up to the mill, after first speaking to him outside.

"Jack's agreed to dress the stones and to show you his metal."

Willingly, this slightly built man rolled up his sleeves, and Dick didn't envy him his job.

40

"See to the brakes Dick and I'll leave you both to it."

He watched transfixed, as this small man hoisted up the huge top stone, revealing the grooves where the flour is ground. Dick was shocked at how big they were and if they fell, Jack would certainly be crushed; no wonder mills are dangerous places, he thought.

He winced; as the sparks flew off the stone embedding themselves into Jack's already scarred arms. While he was grinding the second stone; Molly's high pitched scream made him run as quickly as he dare down the steps, and he left Jack.

"Nay what's wrong lassie?" He panted.

A red eyed Molly pointed to Sam's lifeless body in the chair.

"He looked asleep so I shook him and his head fell on one side, I thought he'd get better."

Dick held her trembling body, and tenderly stroked her long dark hair. He often wished he could have done that, but this was a bad time to leave the mill. Dick was still holding her when a knock came at the door, and it was Parkinson.

"I've done, come and check it before I put it back."

He was loathed to leave her, but Molly insisted.

"Go and watch him Dick and I'll get his money."

On his return, Molly had dried her eyes before paying Jack, who then left. Being an only child she had all the arrangements to make.

"Canna I, help yee?" He enquired.

"Will you get the doctor and the minister, Dick? I don't want to leave Father."

"Aye, I'll go now." On the way he wondered how they buried their dead in England.

After the doctor wrote the death certificate, she made arrangements with the minister to have Sam buried with her mother in the churchyard. Two days

41

later in what was to be a quiet funeral, many farmers and villagers came to pay their respects. It was very different from his parent's simple burials. Things were strained between them after as Molly grieved; Dick felt strange being alone in the house with her.

By June the mill was busy with farmers clearing their granaries and he coped with it. He wondered how bad it would get at Harvest time, as his knee ached already. They worked together amiably, proving that all Molly had taught him had gone in, but eventually he had to speak his mind.

"Molly lassie, I want to say something." He could stand it no longer.

"You're not leaving me Dick, not now?" She gasped.

"Nay, Molly! I want us to get wed; I love yee and hope yee love me?"

"MARRY YOU! I've only just buried my Father!"

"Nay how about after the harvest, what do yee say?" He held his breath.

"We began badly Dick didn't we, but when you stood up to Father, I knew we'd be together. So after the harvest is fine and I 'll wed you then."

It was her first smile since his death.

"I dinna like yee at first; I could have slapped yee for laughing at me. But when yee showed me to yon room and smiled with those lovely eyes, I loved yee then."

They sealed their agreement with a long lingering kiss, the first of many he hoped. He continued to have strange feelings around her, but life became easier after that. But Dick had no idea of what was about to happen in the very near future.

Chapter 4 Robert

Robert was relieved that they had crossed the bridge safely and he was glad that Richard was there. He would be forever indebted to that farmer who was unaware that he had saved their lives, as he nonchalantly whistled tunelessly. It had been a terrifying ordeal escaping as they did, in fact the last few months had been the worst experience of his life. He was devastated leaving Richard at the second crossroads, although he had promised they would meet again one day. But the further he travelled the less convinced he became, and soon he began to feel dejected. Willingly, he had lived in his more dominant brother's shadow, having no confidence in himself. Robert knew it all began with their mother's death and their father's silence until he died. Through all this Richard remained his constant protector and restored his security.

Things changed again after they were forced into this rebellion, armed only with knives and dirks they picked up from their fallen comrades. Each suffered injuries from either a Redcoat's bayonet or musket, Thomas saved all their lives even though he himself was injured. He envied his eldest brother's strength and bravery; he was the only one who could wield the Claymore's double edged sword, which could decapitate a Redcoat at a stroke. He was relieved when they tossed their weapons into the depths of the river today, so they could start new lives as unthreatening men.

Robert walked miserably for miles along the twisting lanes of rural lanes Lancashire; which was so different from the sparse scrubland back home. Eventually he reached a market town where crowds of people milled around countless stalls, which were lined up on each side of the street. There traders sold their wares, this was something he had never seen before and it made him nervous dressed as he was. He wished he had stayed with Richard who would know, but he was alone and scared, and could trust nobody. While passing a dairy stall the delicious smell of cheese made his mouth water, he could hardly remember the last time he ate. He saw to his amazement a young boy steal a piece of cheese from the back of the stall, he too was hungry, but he would never do that.

The irate stallholder, a buxom woman in her forties, he assumed yelled at him.

"Hey you over there, which way did he go?"

Robert was mortified and pointed to the crowd.

"Aye and how did yee ken?" He asked

Winking, she tapped her nose.

"When it's your own stock you get a second sense about it, but that's my profit for the day gone. It's no fun standing here all day in the cold, without brats like that robbing you. Can't get a warm drink, unless you'll get it for me?"

"Nay, how?" Robert gasped.

"Fool, I'll give you the money and get one for yourself too?" She said and thrust the exact amount in his hand; unaware of the grave danger she had put him in. He returned with two bowls of hot broth and handed one to her, which she grabbed.

"Aye thank yee lady."

"Hey, we'll have none of that, I'm Margaret Garner but folks call me Peg. Just because you're from another country don't make you bad, that young thief's bad, if anyone is."

"Aye I'm Robert Mc Cardell."

"I'll call you Bob Cardell, here aren't you one of them there Jakowatsits?"

"Aye a Jacobite but I dinna want to."

"Then get behind them boxes and keep your eyes peeled, in case that thief comes back."

"Thank yee, Peg."

Robert didn't care what she called him as he drank his broth; now warmed and exhausted after his long journey he slept. Only to be awakened by a commotion outside, fearing it was the Redcoats he peeped out. But it was only the traders packing up their stalls.

"Come on Bob, shake a leg and load these boxes." Peg shouted.

She made it sound normal, and he scampered out to help. The wooden boxes were heavy making his shoulder ache, but he persisted. Later when Peg disappeared he feared she had gone to inform the Redcoats about him. But she soon returned leading a horse and attached it to the cart, which had doubled up as the stall.

"Aye that's grand!" He exclaimed, until he saw that all the other traders were doing exactly the same. What had earlier been a thriving market was now a collection of horses and carts, but as the last box was loaded it began to snow.

Peg got on her cart, and glared at him.

"What are you gawping at Bob, unless you want to sleep rough tonight, take a chance and come home with me."

Robert or Bob as he was now called didn't need asking twice and he eagerly jumped up. Peg wore a long heavy gent's coat which only revealed her black leather shoes. Over it she had a white pinny with big pockets for the money. Her ever watchful hazel eyes missed nothing, and on her head she wore a white mobcap.

"Now tell me your story, it'll be ages before we get home?"

He felt she deserved an explanation and he told her everything that had happened.

"Won't your parents worry about you all?"

"Nay they're dead, Thomas and Jinni took over and they were only bairns themselves."

"That'll do for now." Peg wiped a tear from her eye.

"Aye, what will yon man say, about me?"

"James died a few months back and now my kids help me. Jim does the milking and collects the eggs; Dinah helps me to blend the butter and cheese. I get to Bondswick once a week; it's the only way we can make any money."

He felt sorry for her, as he wiped the snow off his ginger hair and beard, as it soaked his already shabby kilt. Peg steered the weary horse down a sodden twisted path towards a farmhouse at the end. Smoke came out of a chimney, their croft didn't have one which why it was called a blackhouse. On their arrival a light shone from the window. Peg alighted and shouted her son.

"Shake a leg Jim and hold the horse while we get this stock in and Bob you can put these boxes in the dairy before we freeze to death? I hope Dinah's made something to eat, we're both starving?"

This matriarch handed out her orders which were complied with. Bob carried the heavy boxes in and they made his shoulder ache, but he didn't care. He put them on an empty stone shelf over a slate floor before dusting the snow off. Their croft floor was only earth and wasn't as big as this dairy, he mused. He noticed a strange looking contraption in one corner and assumed it must be where they made the butter. A second stone shelf ran along the other wall, which he again assumed was where they made the cheese. As he removed the last box, he heard Peg outside issuing more orders.

"See to the horse and cart, Jim."

Bob then heard a pleasant female voice coming from inside the house.

"I bet you're soaked through and ready for something to…" The woman's voice stopped abruptly on seeing him. Fortunately Peg soon returned and explained.

"We are that lass, Dinah this is Bob Cardell, he helped me today and he's come to work for us, Bob this is my daughter."

Her long blonde hair was neatly tied back with a blue ribbon that matched her eyes and pretty dress, it revealed her shapely figure which was in sharp contrast to Peg and Jim's build and colouring; she must look like her father, he assumed once more.

"Pleased to meet you Bob, you're drenched!" She extended her hand and smiled.

"Aye I am lassie and it's grand to meet yee too." He shook her hand and he resembled a drowned rat dripping on the floor, as his clothes clung to his wet body.

"Get your Dad`s clothes Dinah; they'll fit him better than Jim's." Peg ordered again and Bob felt he was being taken over, but he didn't mind so long as he was warm. Suddenly the dairy door flung open and looking extremely disgruntled was Jim.

"Seen to the horse Mum, and who are you?" He glared menacingly

"Bob helped me out this afternoon, so I've asked him to stay. With his help we'll get to the market again before Christmas." Peg explained.

"Before what?" Bob asked.

"Where did you, come from?" Jim sneered.

"Aye, I'm from Skye, so I've nay heard of it?" Bob reacted unusually

Peg briefly explained about Christmas and that presents were exchanged.

"Nay what's a present?" He asked.

"You buy them with money that you'll earn working on the market, so don't fret!" "Aye, but what's money?" He asked again, and Jim continued to sneer.

"I'll show you next time we go to Bondswick, and then we might all have something to open on Christmas day."

"In that case Bob, I'm glad you've come." Jim's attitude then changed realizing that he would benefit and held out a chubby hand which Bob reluctantly shook, but he worried that Jim might tell the Redcoats about him. Dinah soon returned with some clothes.

"Take these Bob, Jim'll show you where to go, I'll fetch some water from the well and a towel so you can wash."

"Follow me." Jim muttered at seeing his father's clothes. Bob trailed behind carrying them up the stairs; he said nothing about never seeing stairs before. At the top Jim took great delight in showing his authority.

"This room here is Mums, that one's Dinah's, this is mine, and you can have this one! You've got nothing with you, so you won't need much room will you?"

Jim was being nasty again and left. Bob was thrilled to have a room and bed of his own.

Later Dinah knocked on his door.

"I've brought Dad's shoes and stockings and his shaving things, I'll get the bowl of water and the towel I left on the landing."

She had Peg's kind nature but was much gentler he thought and accepted them gladly.

"Thank yee, Dinah." Her pretty face smiled before she also left.

Bob completed his ablutions and dressed in the brown corduroy britches that fitted him well as did the claret fustian velvet shirt, the grey stockings and black leather shoes changed his appearance. He was pleased that Peg's husband was the same build as him and felt warmer when he returned downstairs, ignoring Jim's glare about what he wore.

As promised Peg took him to the market next day.

"I'll show you how to set up the stall first and then I'll nip off to barter what I need for home. When we've sold something you can go and get what gifts you want out of your wages, and I'll sort it later with the traders."

Bob nodded and watched in admiration as Peg efficiently plied her trade, he wondered if he would ever be able do it. Later he chose a new mobcap for Peg, a pretty pink ribbon for Dinah and a muffler for Jim to keep him warm while doing the milking in the cold.

Christmas would have been a great experience, had it not been for the miserable Jim. He still worried that if ever the mood took him, he could easily report him to the Redcoats.

*   *   *

Over the next month the atmosphere with Jim became unbearable and Bob spoke to Peg. "I owe yee my life, but I mun be away from here."

"Aren't you happy here, Bob?"

"Aye with yee and Dinah, but its yon Jim that bothers me."

"He's always been jealous, but don't let him drive you away?"

"I can nay do anything with yon man, can I?"

"You can't, but I can, if you and Dinah run the stall, Jim and I will make the stock."

"Aye, but will Dinah nay mind?"

"Never, you've always got on well."

Later Peg explained the arrangements to her daughter and everything improved.

Dinah taught him how to handle money and they worked on the market six days a week. Sunday was the only day they were all together, Dinah did the washing and Peg got the dinner ready.

"Canna I help yee?" Bob asked.

"No, I can manage!" Jim snapped.

Peg heard it as she put the roast in the oven of the black leaded grate over the fire.

"You and Dinah get out in this sunshine; dinner will be a while yet."

Peg informed Dinah when she returned from hanging the washing out.

"Why don't you and Bob have a stroll for a couple of hours?"

"But Mum, it's not right leaving everything to you?"

"Bob can help with the dishes later while you press the clothes; now get off the pair of you, before I change my mind."

Throwing off her wet pinny she quickly brushed her long blonde hair and giggled. "Aren't you sick of seeing me all week, without spending you're day off with me?"

"Nay, you're always in a good mood." He replied.

"Are you sure about that?" She winked.

They left and strolled contentedly down the twisted lane into the village.

"I'll show you my dad's grave, the service should be over by now."

"Aye do yee miss him Dinah?"

"Yes, because we looked alike, but his nature was like Jim's and I didn't like that."

He thought it was strange that Peg and Dinah's natures were alike yet Jim and Peg were built the same.

"Do you miss you're parents, Bob?"

50

"Aye, but I was a wee laddie when both of them died."

Sharing such intimate feelings drew them even closer; Bob began to feel safe again, so long as the miserable Jim kept his distance.

At the market he learned how to barter, and the traders now accepted him. Farmers sold their hay and flour, others brought various cuts of meat, there were stalls selling fruit and vegetables from their smallholdings. One sold men's and ladies clothes, and another sold shoes and stockings, while an elderly lady sold lace and another dried fruits.

"Aye I'll need a cooler shirt and thinner britches for yon hot days."

"And Betty's made me a cotton dress, she's packed away all her hand knitted shawls and mufflers till the winter. Mum wants new shoes and Jim needs a jacket. We've also to get a piece of mutton and vegetables for dinner tomorrow."

Bob found it easy to get on with Dinah and enjoyed every day they spent together. The summer sun gave him a weathered complexion, back on Skye the sun didn't last too long. He thought if John lived down here, his chest would be better. A cold shiver ran down his spine as he remembered about his brothers, that he hadn't thought of for so long.

Life could not have been better as he enjoyed the banter of the market like Peg did. He was sad that she gave it up to keep the peace with the horrid Jim. Bob thought Richard would be proud of him and wondered if he was still alive. But he pushed these thoughts out of his mind because they did not belong in his new life. On a late June afternoon as the market heaved and through the thronging crowds he noticed a familiar face from his past. Reigniting memories he had tried hard to forget. After six months he had given up hope of seeing anyone he knew again, but this person wasn't dressed as at their last meeting.

Chapter 5 Tom

Leaving Blackmoor Moss Alice was flushed from rushing, and Tom thought how lovely she looked in her bright pink floral dress and bonnet. This was the first time he had left the farm and the land around was now transformed into a lush, fertile area. The fields he and Harry had sown were producing a healthy crop of wheat. The cows grazed contentedly in the lush fields and returned twice daily to be milked. Birds were singing while bees and butterflies were busy, on this gloriously sunny June day in 1746.

Reaching the lane he asked.

"Aye which way lassie?"

She gestured to where he first met Harry, he wondered if his fall that day might have caused his back problem.

"Is it far?"

"I wouldn't fancy walking it, why didn't you go when dad asked you?"

"I dinna have the time."

"Dad didn't, but he managed to go."

He hated lying to her and so changed the subject.

"Aye but it's grand round here, isna it?"

"Suppose so, but what's it like up north?"

"It's nay as nice as everywhere in England." He cautiously explained.

"So you've been around, have you?"

"Aye, but only since I left home." This was true.

"Oh I see, but do you miss your home Tom?"

"Nay, I'm settled now, where to next?"

She pointed to where William went.

"Turn here at Queeny Carters cottage and go over the bridge."

He gulped as all the bad memories flooded back, where they threw their stones and tossed their weapons into the turbulent river before parting. Though now the trees were rich in foliage and seabirds sunbathed on the exposed shale banks.

"Aye I bet yee could walk across it today, dinna yee think?"

"Some folks do, but in the winter it's bad!"

He knew that only too well and wondered if Richard and Robert made it, or did the soldiers guarding the Manor kill them.

"Is there nay a mill nearer?"

"Yes, but Dad always comes to Cunningham because as you know he and your mother used to work on a farm there, it's only a few more miles now."

Miles or directions meant nothing to him; he was glad Alice pointed the way, and that Harry had taught him how to count. By the time they got there the mill it was very busy.

"Aye, there's a fair few carts here, I'll ken how they do it."

It was hot so Alice removed her bonnet to waft her face and the sun caught the highlights of her blonde curly hair, tempting him to touch it.

"I hope old Sam's better, Dad said he'd been ill?"

Tom only cared about being with her.

"It's us now; do you want a hand, Tom?"

"Nay, yee hold Daisy steady and I'll unload."

While putting his first sack on the hook a familiar voice shouted down.

"How many sacks?"

He looked up.

"THOMAS! Is that yee?" The man screamed.

"RICHARD! It canna be?" He yelled back

Alice looked on in amazement, as the man dashed down the steps almost losing his balance and bear hugged Tom.

"Nay, Richard why are yee here?" Barely able to believe his eyes he listened intently.

"Aye I work here, but I've nere seen yee afore?"

Before Tom could explain, an attractive woman popped her head out of the mill door.

"It's Thomas, Molly; I told yee he was like a father to us on Skye."

"Stay for something to eat, that's if we ever get finished, get back Dick." She shouted.

"Aye, I'm away now Molly, see yee later Thomas." He laughed

Tom nodded and turning he saw the startled look on Alice's face. He felt guilty she had found out about him, but finished unloading before moving the cart for the next farmer.

"So, Tom, explain to me what's just happened?" She ranted.

"Nay I'm sorry Alice lassie, but yee father dinna want anyone to ken about it."

"My...my father knew and never said anything?" She gasped and got more annoyed.

"Aye the scar on my face dinna come from the cart; it was from a Redcoat's bayonet. Yee father ken I was a Jacobite after I helped him. If they'd found me, he'd have suffered too, so his story gave me a new life."

She was agog as he got down from the cart.

"Aye, I'll away for the flour and yee father's money."

She let him go to sort out his business. After conducting it, he told Dick everything.

"Aye and now Alice hates me."

He was unaware that she was now standing behind him.

55

"I don't hate you, Tom." Tears fell from face and he dashed over to her.

"So, I ken yee are joining us for dinner?" Dick enquired.

Tom nodded.

"Yes, please." She sniffed.

Holding her trembling hand he introduced her.

"Alice lassie, this is my brother Dick."

"Grand to meet yee Alice and this is Molly, the Miller."

"Glad to meet you both, but I'm sorry, has something happened to your father?"

Molly nodded sadly, explaining that he'd died, before showing them into the house.

Alice took their bagging in to help with the food, and they left the brothers to talk.

"I canna believe we've found each other, so how've yee been?" Dick asked.

"Aye, my scars have healed but the memories dinna, but how's yon leg?"

"Yee ken it nearly gave way, but it'll nay be right again? I have nightmares, do yee?"

"Aye, I wake up seeing all yon bodies bleeding and dying. We passed the river and the tide was low and we could have walked across it."

"Where did yee away to?"

Tom explained everything.

"So yee've nay seen, wee William, then?"

"Nay, have yee seen, Robert, yet?"

"Nay, I've only been to yon village with Molly to get work clothes to fit me. Yee should have seen me on that first day in her father's clothes they almost drowned me."

"Nay not like me in Harry's, they were too short and tight." They laughed, completely at ease together until Tom explained.

"We canna stay long; we're away to the market after."

"Aye, that'll be Bondswick market, Molly wanted to take me but dinna want to leave her father who was dying. She's in shock, but it was worse losing our mother for us."

Dick saw how sad Tom looked and so he changed the subject.

"We're getting wed after the harvest; Molly's an only bairn, say yee'll come?"

"Aye, and I'm sure Alice will too, we'll ask her when they come back in."

The four of them ate and it was agreed that they would return for the wedding.

"Will yee, be my best man, Thomas?"

"Nay Thomas canna, but Tom will." He joked enjoying their time together.

Later, Dick and Molly waved them off.

"Aye are we grand now Alice lassie?" He questioned unable to take his eyes off her.

"Yes, but we've to tell Mum, I've never kept anything from my parents."

"Aye, we will, yee ken Alice, I've loved yee from the day we met."

"That's when I fell for you in my Dad's old clothes."

"Aye and if yon man dinna hurt his back, all this canna have happened."

She smiled back and pointed the way, as they arrived he tethered Daisy to a post, and they searched through the stalls. From behind one of them, someone shouted his name. "THOMAS MC CARDELL?" Running towards him was another young man, who also bear hugged him.

"Aye ROBERT! What are yee doing here?"

"I work on yon stall, fancy seeing yee, yon scars hidden under that beard, how are yee?"

"Aye the scar dinna bother me, but how's yon shoulder?"

"Nay it only hurts when it's cold or if I lift things, but the mind hurts."

"Aye and I've lots to tell yee Robert, but yee mun meet Alice, this is Robert, my brother, she's Harry Hock's daughter who took me in."

After shaking hands, a feisty young fair haired woman rampaged from behind the stall. "His names Bob! And I'm Dinah Garner; he lives with us at our farm."

"Aye and I'm Tom, its odd how all our names are cut short, even Dick`s."

"Nay, yee've nere seen Richard, I mean Dick?"

"Aye, we've just left him and have I got news for yee."

While they talked, Dinah showed Alice where the dried fruit stall was and then quickly returned to her stall. When Alice arrived back the men were acting like children, while Dinah dealt with a long line of customers and urgently shouted for Bob.

"Aye and will yee both come to the wedding Bob, Dick will be keen, to see yee?"

"Dinah will ken the way, aye it's good seeing yee, and I canna wait to see Dick again."

Leaving them, Tom and Alice began the journey home. Reaching the river again they stopped, and getting down Tom explained.

"Aye lassie so many brave warriors drowned there and it's here we left each other, William went the other way from me." He looked in his direction, and Alice tenderly kissed his cheek. It sent shivers down his spine and he respond by kissing her back. They were soon rolling on the lush grass entwined in each others arms.

Their emotions carrying them to such heights they were swept along in their passion for each other. Eventually lying there completely sated, nothing seemed important any more. He could not believe that in only six month his life had changed, he was in love and loved back.

"Oh Tom! We've to go or it'll be dark before we get home."

Alice shrieked as they hurriedly dressed.

"Aye, the first day I leave yon farm and my life's turned upside down."

Cuddling her again before they set off, it was later that he noticed how quiet she was.

"Yee're nay sorry about what we've done, are yee Alice?"

"No, but I'm worried what Mum will say about being lied to."

"Aye, she'll ken why Harry made up yon story."

"We'll soon know."

As they turned down the cinder path into the dark yard, a light shone from the house. "Yee take the fruit in and dinna say a word until I've settled Daisy down."

He was soon back and gave the flour to Maggie and Alice in the kitchen, before going to see how Harry was and to give him the money for the grain.

"How did you go on, Tom lad?" Harry shuffled on the settle.

"Nay old Sam's dead and Molly's now the Miller, my brother Dick works there. They're getting wed after the harvest, Alice is going, I'm his best man, but that's nay all."

Harry visibly paled seeing Maggie flushed with anger.

"Don't stop Tom, do go on?"

Tom had never seen this side of her as she was usually such a placid woman.

"Nay I'm sorry Maggie, but I was a Jacobite fleeing from the Redcoats. After helping Harry, he made up the story, so dinna be angry, he's a brave man."

Maggie still vented her wrath, on her shamefaced husband.

"Why didn't you trust me, all our married life we've always been honest?"

"Would you have felt the same about Tom, if you'd known Mum?" Alice enquired.

She knew Tom's fear about being found out.

"You may as well know too, that we love each other and have ever since we met. I was angry at first when I found out, but now we're free to love each other."

She reached for Tom's hand to confirm that she and Harry were on his side.

"Maybe not, but I'm hurt that you didn't tell me Harry?" Maggie admitted.

He struggled to his feet and placed and apologetic arm around her. After accepting it they listened to how Tom, also met Bob at the market.

"So tell me Tom, what about the rest of your family?"

"Aye well my parents' families dinna get on, that's why we lived on the highlands. When our mother died in childbirth…"These words made him gulp.

"What happened then?" Maggie urged.

"Father was nay the same after so at twelve I took over, Jinni at eleven ran the house and looked after him until he died. John, our sick brother saw to the bairns; it was hard for the seven of us as we were only bairns too." He gulped.

"What a sad life you've had, Tom."

Alice comforted him, and as the women waited with baited breath. Harry hobbled to the settle to rest; he'd heard it all before.

"Where are the highlands?" Maggie enquired.

"Aye it's a wee island called Skye near Scotland, but we dinna ken that till later."

"Oh Tom! But I'm glad you found two brothers and I hope you find the other one too. It'll be nice having them all here when you do get wed."

"Aye, it will? We're lucky to have lived after all that fighting. But those back home canna be there and they'll nay ken about it."

"So that scar on your face, wasn't from the cart then?" Maggie remembered.

"Nay it was from a Redcoat's bayonet, but I got off lightly."

"Why, what happened to the others?" She questioned

"Dick was shot in the leg and still limps. Bob was shot in the shoulder and they'd have bled to death till I removed the shots, with a dirk I found."

" What's a dirk, Tom?" Maggie gasped.

"It's a dagger worn by the clan leaders."

She grimaced.

"Let's not think about that, just think about what will happen." Alice comforted him.

"We'd best get to bed it's late, we'll be fit for nothing tomorrow." Maggie said.

Harry looked exhausted so Tom put him into bed; Alice went to her room and he would have liked to have joined her, but didn't.

It was late July before they had chance to make love again. Each time Harry went delivering the milk, they could not keep away from each other. By the end of September and the harvest was over, Alice broke her heart to him in the barn.

"What's wrong lassie?" He had never seen her cry; she was normally such a happy girl.

"We've reaped our own harvest, Tom, I'm with child." She sobbed.

61

"Nay are yee sure?" Tom gulped; a cold sweat ran down his neck remembering his mother died in childbirth. He knew how his father had felt losing his mother so young.

"What shall we do?"

"Aye we'll get wed."

"But, what'll my parents, say?"

He was worried but had no choice, so they faced them together.

"Aye Maggie where are yee?" He shouted nervously.

"Making the wedding cake and keeping Harry's hands out of the bowl, why?"

"Is there enough mix for two cakes, Mum?" Alice asked.

"Why, whatever for?" Maggie questioned with flour on her nose and saw Alice upset. "What's the matter lass, why do you want another cake?"

Harry peeped from behind her.

"Aye, we'll need one sooner than we thought." Tom stated.

"Not yet surely, there's no rush, is there?"

Alice broke down and Tom put his arm around her.

"Aye there is Maggie, we are having a bairn."

"Does that mean that you've got our Alice in trouble, Tom?" Harry ranted.

"We got in trouble together, Dad, so don't just blame him!"

"I trusted you and after all we've done for you, this how you repay us?" Harry persisted.

"It's nay to do with trust Harry; we love each other and want to wed. It's just sooner than we thought, that's all, I'm sorry if I've let yee down."

"How far gone are you, lass?" Maggie questioned.

"About two months, I think Mum?"

Tom had expected Maggie to be much worse.

"In that case, you can get married the month after Dick and Molly. We'd best get the church booked, Harry will you take Tom, to see the minister?"

"Is that all you've to say, Maggie?" Harry gasped.

Ignoring her husband, Maggie wiped her hands on her pinny and kissed Alice's cheek. "You won't be the first lass and I'm damn sure you won't be the last, to get into trouble. I won't pretend to be pleased about it, but it happens to the best of us. At least you'll be spared the shame of having a child without its father's name." Maggie glared at Harry.

"You'd both best go and sort out a wedding, Alice can help me to mix more cake."

They made themselves presentable and left to see the minister. The atmosphere between them was strained, until reaching the church.

"You'll have guessed from Maggie's words it can happen to the best of us."

Tom shrugged, but his mind was still bothered by Maggie's words.

"I was cross my lass is having a child it makes me feel old. I know you love her and I'm sorry for just blaming you."

"Aye, and I'll be good to her." Tom added.

"See that you are!" Harry warned.

The wedding was arranged, Tom didn't tell Harry his fears, and kept them to himself.

On their return, Alice dashed out with flour all up her slender arms eager to know.

"What's the Vicar say?"

Maggie listened from the kitchen door and Harry joined her.

"Aye it's the last Sunday in November at one o clock."

Alice flung her arms around his neck.

"We'll be ready, won't we, Mum?"

63

"Yes, if we get this cake done and we'll sort out the rest later."

If Maggie appeared to be unworried she did a good job.

"Think those two bullocks should go to market, let's go lad?"

"Aye I'll give yee a hand Harry."

When it was done they grabbed some bagging and were relieved to be on the road.

"Are we away to get anything, Harry?"

"Don't need to, I just thought we 'd best get out the way."

It was a bright autumn day as they set out for the auction, and the leaves were changing colour and ready to fall off the trees.

"Aye and how was it when yee got wed, Harry?"

"Much the same, all rushed and over in no time."

"Yee nay sorry yee wed, Maggie?"

Harry shrugged, as he changed direction.

"No, she's a good wife, so if you're worried about our Alice, she's a good one too."

Tom saw the road they had taken, was the one William had gone down. A few miles down the road was the auction, and they left the bullocks with the market manager who gave Harry a number, before they entered the arena. Tom could not believe how fast the auctioneer spoke, as the animals were led into the ring a few at a time.

"Don't move a muscle, Tom, or he'll think you're bidding."

He sat down too scared to breathe, until someone poked him in his back. Turning angrily, he could not believe that behind him was young William. Jumping up in surprise he grabbed his brother's hand, shouting in delight. "WILLIAM! It canna be?"

"Get outside, or we'll end up buying our own bullocks back!" Harry bellowed.

They rushed outside hugging each other wildly.

"Aye what are yee, doing here?" They shouted in unison.

"Yee first William, and how's yee side?"

"Nay it was bad and hurt for a long time but the scar will nere go or the nightmares."

"Aye, I ken what yee mean, Dick still limps and Bob's shoulder aches when it's cold."

"Nay yee met them, Thomas, so they're alive." William beamed.

"Aye, I'll tell yee all, after yee tell me about what happened to yee."

William explained and also that Agnes had died and was buried in a coffin in the churchyard on top of her parents."

"Nay, they canna ken who was buried there?"

"Aye they dig a deep grave first and a gravestone has their name and date of death on it, and again for each one after?"

"Nay, do folks read, there?" Tom gasped.

"Aye, some do, Emily the vicar's daughter taught me, and now she's my young lassie. Yee'd nay believe it Tom, but I'm a member of the Church of England."

"Dinna think a Scot would get in the Kirk of England?"

"Aye, they let me, I go to the kirk on Sunday, when I take the ladies."

"Yee clever laddie, I ken yee'd do well and I'm proud on yee." Tom hugged him. "Aye and I'm sorry about Agnes, but yon Emily's a clever lassie, teaching yee to read."

"Aye she is, now what about yee?"

Tom explained all about Harry and Alice first and then mentioned. "Dick's getting wed in October at

Cunningham Kirk. Bob's coming, canna yee come too?"

"Are all yon names shortened?"

"Aye, I'm now Tom, what about yee?"

"Nay I'm still William, but just Cardell now."

"Aye we're all Cardells now, isna that strange?"

He didn't finish the story as Harry and Martha came out of the auction, and they were all introduced. William told Martha, about Dick's wedding, but she looked downcast still being in mourning.

"I canna leave the ladies yet, Tom, but I'd love to meet them all again."

"Come to our Alice and Tom's wedding, it's on the last Sunday of November in Blackmoor Church at one o clock? Bring the ladies and your Emily."

Harry took the words out of his mouth, but Tom had the last word.

"Aye, William I need a best man; will yee be it?"

"Yes, we'd love to come to your wedding, Tom, but as for being your best man it's up to William?" Martha answered and smiled at him like he was her son.

"Then, aye, I'll be yon best man, Tom, and Emily will love to meet my brothers. She kens all about them, especially yee, Tom. But we must away and pick up what we've bought; we'll see yee all in November."

Leaving William this time was all right, as Tom knew they would all meet again soon.

"You'd best get them four shorthorn calves on the cart, big lad."

"Yee dinna buy them Harry?"

"I didn't, you did when you jumped up, I told you to keep still." Harry laughed.

"Aye but, I've nay money with me?"

"The bullocks covered it; you can pay me when we get home."

"Aye, I will Harry, I wanted to get Alice a wedding present."

"It's a damned dear present; you'll need a bull as mine won't do." He laughed again.

"Nay, why not?"

Harry shook his head in amusement. But not even the prospect buying a new bull, could spoil Tom's delight at seeing William again.

As they returned Harry ran to fetch Alice, who arrived wondering what was wrong.

"I've met William! Aye and he's my best man, his young lassie Emily and the Bradman sisters he works for are all coming to the wedding. Now lassie, come and see yon wedding present."

"I'm so glad you've met William, but what wedding present?"

He removed the cover off the calves, and Alice's face lit up.

"Ah! They're beautiful thank you Tom, but I've nothing to give you."

She then kissed him so hard that it nearly broke his neck.

"Aye, that's my present, the other comes next year; they're nay like yon dad's cows."

They settled them into the calving pen, as Alice stroked their faces they licked her hand.

"These are the start of the Mr and Mrs Tom Cardell's herd, I'll call them Alice, Molly, Dinah, and Emily."

"Aye, let's hope they'll all be Cardells?" Later they went into the house.

Next day he and Harry took the first load of grain to the mill, and queued up with all the other farmers.

<u>Chapter 6 William</u>

William enjoyed the happiest summer of his life with Emily at Freestone.

In September he and Martha took a cow to the auction, Ruth remained to milk the others.

It was an eventful day and he was ecstatic at meeting his brother and finding out that his other brothers were also safe.

"Well, fancy you meeting Tom, and he's just like you described him, whatever will Ruth say when we tell her?"

"Aye she's at the gate, but dinna say anything until I've put the cart away."

"You look pleased with yourselves, was it a good day?" Ruth asked as Martha alighted.

"Good isn't close, have we got something to tell you?"

He smiled, and on his return Ruth enquired.

"Is Tom, as handsome as you William?"

"Aye but he's bigger and stronger, a gentle giant and yee'll love him." He blushed.

Ruth continued while serving a meat pie that she had baked earlier.

"If he's half the man you are, I'm sure I will."

"When we've eaten, I'm away to tell Emily, the news."

He rushed out and eagerly knocked on the vicarage door, he saw that Emily had been crying as she opened it.

"Nay lassie what ails yee?"

"Let us go for a walk William, I have something to tell you." She sniffed.

"Aye and I've got things to tell yee, Emily, but it can wait."

"Squire Markham the church's patron wants his son, James, to be the new vicar. He said a Squire at Eastrick needs one, and that my father must accept the post." She wept.

"Yee dinna have to go, do yee?"

"The Squire expects his son to move in at the end of the month."

"Nay, but why?"

"The first born inherits the estate; the second joins the army, the third is a minister."

"But, canna yee stay?"

"I have to go with my father."

"Canna yee live with us and have Agnes's room?"

"I have no income, so I must go." She sobbed.

"Dinna do anything, until I've spoken to Ruth and Martha."

"But, we have already started to pack." She sighed.

"Aye but I'll take yee home now, and I'll be back soon." He turned to leave. .

"But William you never told me what you were going to say?"

"Nay, I'll tell yee later, just trust me."

Arriving back red faced, he shocked the sisters and Martha gasped.

"What's the matter, William, you look like you've seen a ghost."

He quickly explained everything.

"She can stay, but we can't keep her, as there isn't enough money." Ruth replied.

"Emily can earn money teaching children to read, can't she?" Martha suggested.

"Aye, she can use the outhouse for a classroom?" William volunteered.

"Where will you sleep, there's no more bedrooms?" Ruth queried.

"We'll get wed, and have Agnes's room, what do yee think?"

"Oh, just like that? If she'll marry you and if her father allows it?" Martha added.

"Aye, but if she stays, I'll ask her father to let us wed if he dinna allow it, I'll go too."

"Think about it, William, getting married takes time to arrange." Ruth reminded him.

"There's nay time, they're packing now."

He ran to the vicarage to put his plan into action, knocking loudly at the door, startling Emily in the process.

"Will yee wed me, Emily? We'll live at the cottage and open a school in the outhouse; say aye, so I can ask yon father?"

"I would love to marry you, William, but what will Father say? Besides, opening a school will take time to organise."

"Aye, yee've the books, and canna we move them now. If yon father agrees, he can marry us afore he's away to his new parish, canna he?"

"You have it all sorted out, William, but do the ladies agree?"

"Aye, I said that if yon father dinna agree, then I will go with yee."

"You are so special, William, we will speak to Father now."

They returned to the vicarage and Reverend Parker was astounded.

"Emily is coming with me; personally I would prefer her to wait and not rush into marriage, and besides you have no security to offer her."

"Aye but, we love each other, and we'll live at the Bradmans." He pleaded.

"I have always been obedient to your wishes Father, but you have a housekeeper there, and I would be heartbroken to leave William, so please give us your blessing?"

The Reverend considered it for a while before he answered.

"Very well, but I shall miss you Emily, so you have my blessing. Your marriage will be at the end of the month to allow time for the banns to be read, this will be my last duty at this parish."

"Thank you, Father." Emily hugged him.

"Aye thanks, Reverend." William shook his hand.

"You should inform the Bradmans about this wedding."

They left and on the way to the cottage Emily remembered.

"You never told me your news, William?"

"Aye, I met Tom, at the auction; he's getting wed at the end of November. I'm his best man and yee and the ladies are invited."

"Oh how lovely; will he be your best man?"

"Nay, he's Dick's best man then and Bob's giving Molly away, so we'll ask Ruth and Martha to stand for us."

"What a shame, but it will be nice to share our day with them."

Laughing and undaunted they arrived at the cottage to shock them with their news.

"We've a wedding to plan, Agnes's room to clear, besides a school to prepare, my minds in a whirl." Martha panicked.

"You want me to be best woman William; I've never heard anything like it?" Ruth said.

"Father says anyone can be a witness, which is all a best man is."

"Are you sure Emily that you want an old maid like me as your bridesmaid?"

"Yes, Martha, and just wear your normal clothes because I have no wedding dress. Father gave Mother's away to the poor, after she died. "

"Aye, we want you both, to be part of our wedding." William insisted.

"Can't Tom, be your best man?" Ruth questioned.

"Nay, he's Dick's on that day, remember Martha yee said it was too soon to go? We're only getting wed so I dinna lose Emily."

"Do not forget, William, it is also because we love each other."

"Aye, I've told them that already, Emily lassie."

The sister's spirits were restored.

"What, shall we do first, Ruth?"

"We'll clear Agnes's room, and leave all our sad thoughts behind us."

"Aye but we've to help the Reverend finish packing, but I'll do the heavy lifting later." William explained.

He and Emily then set out for the vicarage hand in hand.

"I am glad our wedding is Father's last duty, but there is so much to do before that."

"Aye and we'll help him, so dinna worry Emily lassie."

As they entered the vestry the Reverend was frowning at a letter.

"Is anything wrong, Father?"

"The Squire wants the stockroom emptying and the contents disposed of. James Markham wants his housekeeper to live there. I have no idea when I can get round to it."

"Aye, I'll help, if yee like?"

"Thank you, William, but what will you do with goodness knows what is in there?"

"Have you the key Father and we can start right now?"

They controlled their excitement unlocking the door and entered.

"Look at all these dusty benches, tables, slates and chalks, everything that we need for the school." Emily gasped.

"Aye, I'll get the cart, and take them to the outhouse."

"You must make room first, and then we need help to lift them?"

"Nay yon father's too busy, and I dinna ken anyone."

"I will ask Mr Jackson the deacon, he will help us."

"I'll away to make room, and bring the cart back."

They hurried off in different directions, eager to get everything done as soon as possible.

On his return, Emily was in the storeroom with a powerfully built man, who he thought looked how Tom might at his age.

"William, this is Mr Jackson the deacon."

"Call me Charlie; now let's get all this on to your cart William." They shook hands and worked hard all morning together; Emily put the smaller items in the vicar's carriage. They were about to leave, when a woman's voice called.

"Wait! The Reverend has asked me to make you all something to eat."

"Thank you, Mary; we could all do with a break."

There was no resistance from the men, and they all trooped into the vestry.

"I'll clean the stockroom for you, and the children can help you to clean everything before it goes into the outhouse." Mrs Jackson suggested. Mary was Charles's wife and a formidable and capable housekeeper.

"Thank you, Mary, any help is most welcome."

After they had eaten they all left. William and Charlie set off with cart. While the bushy haired, freckled face James aged six and Ann a petite brown platted haired five year old joined Emily in her father's carriage each armed with buckets and cloths.

Meanwhile back at the cottage Ruth and Martha were outside waiting for them.

"William, your bed's under the window and we've dragged Father's chest into the house, everything else is in the corner."

"Aye thanks ladies, but the bairns need water, everything is dirty."

Everyone was organised, William, Charlie and James got the heavy things off the cart, and the women cleaned them ready to go inside.

"What's it all for, Miss Emily?" Ann asked.

"I am opening a school, would you and James like to come?"

"If our parents can afford it, Miss."

"Do not worry about it; do you know any other children who will come?"

"I'll ask them, Miss? But, where will Mr William sleep when it opens?"

"We will marry and live with the ladies in the cottage."

"Is the new vicar doing it, or your father?"

"Yes Ann, my father is doing it as you say before he leaves."

"Is he going far away?" Ann persisted.

"I am afraid that he is, Ann."

"Won't you see him again?" Ann continued.

"I do not think so." She realised then, the price she was paying. William's voice brought her back.

"Aye come see what it looks like, Emily lassie."

"Later William, I must get the children home and make Father's meal."

Emily was close to tears as they went and this left William and the ladies in shock.

"Come and have something to eat William, and we'll all have an early night."

He tossed and turned all night and was up early to do the milking, the crisp morning air revived him, before returning to the cottage.

"Breakfasts ready, William, you were up early, is anything wrong?" Martha asked.

"Nay, just needed some fresh air, it's hot in yon place with everything around."

"I've been thinking about Emily, she's had so much on her mind lately, that she might have forgotten about her father leaving." Ruth suggested.

"Aye, Ruth, that's what it'll be, I'm away to see her now."

He dashed to the vicarage and as Emily opened the door she kissed him.

"I am sorry about last night, William, I realised that I might never see my father again."

"Nay lassie, dinna yee want to stay?"

"Yes, because I love you William, and we will be married soon, that is what I want."

Ruth and Martha had filled the hallway with boxes, when William and Emily arrived at the cottage in the vicar's carriage with her personal belongings.

"Aye and what's, all this?" He asked

"They're Agnes's, for the poor; can your father find a home for them?"

"I'm sure he can, Ruth, as soon as we have emptied the carriage." Emily smiled

"Leave everything for the moment; I've made a pot of herbal tea." Martha said.

While they were drinking it Ruth had something on her mind.

"In Agnes's, room we found her unused wedding dress." She casually mentioned.

There was a pause, before Emily enquired. "May I, look at it?"

"I hoped you would!" Ruth beamed and the two women eagerly went upstairs.

"We'll get Emily's things in, and then put these boxes on the cart William."

"We canna fit them in the outhouse Martha, it's full."

"Ruth and I thought you could have the parlour after the wedding."

"Aye yee're so good to us Martha, Emily will be pleased, I dinna ken why any man has nay snapped yee up afore now?"

"If they had, you'd never have met me. I hope you don't mind me asking, but would it upset you if Emily wears Agnes's wedding dress?"

"Nay, not if the lassie likes it and it fits."

All the books were in the parlour, and the last of Agnes's boxes were in the carriage, when Ruth and Emily came triumphantly down the stairs carrying a large package.

"It looks like you'll be wearing a wedding dress, after all, Emily." Martha asked.

"Aye, but are yee sure about this, Emily lassie?" He enquired.

"Yes, William, maybe it was supposed to be for me as it fits so well."

"She looks beautiful in it William, but you've to wait, no peeking." Ruth joked.

She was back to her jovial self again, and it pleased him.

"Ruth and Martha want us to have the parlour after we're wed, what about that Emily?"

"How kind of them and I am sure we will all get along very well."

"I shall have to make an effort now as your bridesmaid, maybe young Ann would like to be one too?" Martha suggested.

"What a lovely idea, but it is a little late for Mary to get her ready."

"Don't worry about that Emily, I can run something up for Ann, and Martha."

"Thank you, Ruth; if you buy the material, then I will pay you."

"I found some blue satin in Agnes's room, so don't worry." She explained.

Emily nodded, and they left for the vicarage with the parcel held tightly on her knee.

A few days later on a bright October morning, the wedding day arrived. Martha spent the previous night at the vestry, to help Ann and Emily with their dresses.

William and Ruth arrived suitably attired, and on entering the church he gasped.

"I dinna expect so many folk to be here, did yee Ruth?"

"They've probably come to wish Reverend Parker well, at the same time."

They took their places near the altar and waited.

"Emily, you look beautiful." Mr Jackson whispered outside the church.

"Thank, you very much, Charles, and also for giving me away."

The organ began and she floated down the aisle on his arm, radiant in her long sleeved, scooped necked, tight waisted, white silk wedding dress with a flowing skirt.

William turned and she took his breath away, he asked a frightened Ruth by his side.

"Nay, was Agnes really going to wear that dress?"

"She wasn't always old; she was an attractive young woman, William."

Emily reached him and Charles handed her over and sat with his wife and son James. Martha took her flowers then she and Ann stood at her side as Reverend Parker began the service. He reached the important part.

"Do you, William Cardell, take Emily Parker, to be your lawful wedded wife?"

Before replying, he thought about Dick saying his vows at the same time, watched over by his two brothers and for a just a moment, he wished they were all there.

After the ceremony Reverend Parker proudly said. "I now pronounce that you are man and wife, you may kiss the bride?"

The congregation applauded them, and also Reverend Parker. Her father's smile assured her that they were both making the right decision.

"Must you go now Father; I thought you had wait for Reverend Markham to come?"

"I do, but Mrs Jackson has prepared something special, if William will escort you and our guests into the vicarage, there is a surprise celebration?"

William thought his heart would burst with joy as the party began. Unfortunately it was abruptly halted by the presence of severe faced Reverend Markham and his well dressed haughty looking wife. His face was flushed with anger at what was happening. Reverend Parker offered a welcoming hand, which was angrily ignored.

"Please excuse us Reverend Markham, but it is my daughter's wedding day, and I was combining it with a farewell to my friends and parishioners. Mrs Jackson will clear it away in no time, unless of course you and your lady wife would care to join us?"

"Indeed not sir, this is no longer your vicarage and I insist that you all leave immediately! I can see there will have to be some drastic changes made around here. You had better be on your way Reverend Parker to your new parish."

"You are quite right sir; I and my guests are now in urgent need of some clean fresh air!" He led the wedding party outside.

"I wish you were not going so far Father and thank you for everything you have done."

"Life changes for all of us my dear; I know that you and William will be happy in your new life, as no doubt will I. Though my job takes me far away, know that your mother would have been so proud of you today."

He kissed her head affectionately and shook Williams's hand before driving away, to the cheers and good wishes of his parishioners. Young Ann in distress went back to her parents for some comfort for missing the party.

William and Emily returned home subdued with Ruth and Martha, though they did have the parlour they all still ate together. William was happy and knew that he would never be alone again. He continued with the milking and to sell their produce in Lymouth, while Emily opened up the school. Mary Jackson brought James and Ann, and some other ladies from the church brought their children. Poorer children also arrived who were unable to pay the fee for their lessons. They brought eggs or fruit and vegetables from their smallholdings instead, which saved the expense of buying them.

"Aye and how was yon first day, Emily?" William enquired.

"Teaching you in the evening was easy, but this is very different."

Ruth put out the meal while she and Martha waited for her reply.

79

"They know nothing, which is why they have all come, but I will have to manage."

I've nay much time lassie, but I'll help if yee like?"

"That is kind of you, William, but it is not enough." She smiled

"I've got some time, and I can read and write." Martha offered.

"Thank you Martha, then perhaps you can help the little ones, and I can take the others?"

"I will and everyone should learn to read and write, Father taught us?" Martha added.

Things improved, William on his deliveries passed the word and more children came.

Before long it was time to set off for Tom and Alice wedding.

"Emily yee do look bonnie as always, aye and so do yee ladies."

She blushed, while sitting next to him on the Sunday carriage, all three were eager to meet his brothers.

"We'll nay pass the river to get to the church, will we, Emily?"

"You said that Tom left you after leaving river, didn't you?"

"Aye so we did, but I dinna fancy seeing it again remembering those who drowned and all the others who were butchered on the battlefields. Our injuries dinna compare to that, yee must have been afeared hearing my nightmares?"

"I understand what you went through."

"Aye and my brothers will be surprised to ken that we're wed."

At the crossroads his spirit lifted, seeing Tom in his wedding clothes waiting for them.

Chapter 7 Dick

Earlier at Cunningham Dick was overjoyed to have met Tom, and that he had agreed to be his best man. But there was little time to dwell on it, as Molly had more to explain about the mill.

"You'd better take note, Dick that besides the farmers, the villagers with no money also need flour."

"Aye and what happens then lassie?"

"I barter with them, for fruit, vegetables, maybe chickens and eggs. Some smallholder offer sides of bacon or a joint off a cow they might have slaughtered, it eases our food bill. Travellers also come in their garish coloured wagons; they exchange their gold jewellery for flour. Later, I'll show you the box under my bed, where we keep them and those my Father took too."

"Aye and what, do yee do with them?"

"Father, called it our rainy day fund."

"I dinna ken, about that?"

"If ever the crops should fail, we can sell some until things improve."

"We dinna have anything for a rainy day on the croft."

The following Sunday, when the last farmer had gone, they came down the mill steps for their midday meal, when a cart arrived, and a voice shouted. "AYE, DICK!"

He turned, and in amazement saw it was his closest brother, with a young lady. He ran tenuously towards him, and in excitement shouted. "ROBERT! How did yee find me?"

"Tom came to Bondswick market; we run a stall for Peg Garner who took me in. This is her daughter Dinah, we work together and she showed me the way."

"Aye, Dinah, I'm Dick, and this is Molly the Miller, and my future wife."

"At last we meet,Bob's told me all about you, and it's nice to meet you too, Molly."

The introductions over, Dinah enquired. "I expected a man to be the Miller?"

"Yes it was, but my Father died." She swallowed hard

"Oh! I'm so sorry!" Dinah gasped.

"Thank you; now let's go in for something to eat, so we can get to know each other?" The women scurried into the kitchen, leaving the brothers to catch up.

"Aye and how've yee been, Bob, and what about yon shoulder?"

"Aye it hurts when it's cold, or if I lift anything heavy. I see your leg still bothers yee?"

"Nay it'll nere be right again, but I cope with it."

"And how did yee get here, Dick?"

"Luck, in taking the right road. But Molly's father put me through it, to get the job. So how did yee meet Peg?"

"Luck again; I was in the right place at the right time. But her son Jim hated me, and I was afeared that he'd tell the Redcoats where I was."

"Dinah seems a nice lassie, are yee two more than friends?"

At that moment, the women brought the food in, and Dick noticed Molly's eyes were red, so he changed the subject, and talked about their wedding.

"Bob laddie, I'd asked Tom, to be my best man, but if we'd met first yee'd be it."

"Aye I know, but Tom's pleased, and I'm just glad to be here."

"Will you give me away, Bob, in place of my Father?"

"Aye Molly, if that's what yee want."

"And will you Dinah, be my bridesmaid, please say yes?"

"Oh! Molly, thanks, I never thought I'd get the chance."

"Come and see my wedding dress? Granny crocheted it for Mother; it's all I've got left of hers."

The women then went upstairs into Molly's bedroom.

"It's beautiful; those lacy flowers look almost real to the touch. I've never seen anything like it! Betty, on the market can make me something, but it'll not be as nice as yours."

That'd be nice, but you look lovely in what you have on now."

"Thanks, Betty made it, but I don't get much chance to wear it."

"Pick what colour you want, and I'm sure it'll look lovely."

They came down and all talked amiably, agreeing to come every Sunday.

Time flew, and Dinah suggested.

"We should go, Bob, we've an early start tomorrow."

"Aye yee're right lassie, it'll be late when we get back."

"Never mind, we'll see you every Sunday, until the harvest time that is. Dick has no idea how busy it gets, he might change his mind about staying."

"Nay I'm nere afeard of hard work lassie, if yon can do it, so can I."

Molly gave them an affectionate hug, before waving them off.

When she returned she explained.

"Dinah knew why I was upset about my Father, she's lost hers too."

After tidying up, they went to bed in their separate rooms, Molly, wanted to wear her white wedding dress honestly.

Just as she predicted, harvest time was indeed hectic. Tom and Harry, were amongst the first to bring their new crop of grain. Harry, sorted out his business with Molly, and offered her his condolences.

"Sam was a good man, I'm sure you'll do as well."

"Thanks, Harry, and it's nice to see you again."

"Tom and Alice, are to wed in November, will you come?"

"We'd love to, but only if you come to ours first? It'll be nice having you all there."

They shook hands on it, before he mentioned.

"Maggie's made your wedding cake."

"Then, I insist that you take an extra sack of flour free."

Dick chatted to Tom by the cart.

"Aye Bob and Dinah, come on Sundays, but with the harvest, we'll nay see them till the wedding. If yee and Alice come we'll be together?"

"Nay we've too much to do, just now, Dick."

"Have yee seen wee William, yet?"

"Aye, I met him at the auction yesterday."

"Nay is he all right?"

"Aye he's all right! He can read, and is courting Emily, the vicar's daughter."

"Nay him reading and is with a vicar's daughter, what next?"

"Aye yee'll nay believe it, he's a member of the Kirk of England."

"Nay, not after we fought against them for so long."

"Aye but he canna come to yon wedding, as the sisters he lives with are mourning their older sister's death. But, he's to be my best man at the end of

November, and he's bringing Emily, and the Bradmans."

"Nay, yee're getting wed, and yee never said a word."

"Aye, we stopped by the river after meeting yee and Bob, and things just happened."

"Yee'd have wed anyway, wait till I tell Bob we'll all be together at last."

The conversation stopped, as Harry arrived and tossed two sacks of flour onto the cart, before joining Tom.

"See yee at the wedding, Dick, Molly`s asked us to come."

"Aye, I'll see yee all then."

Waving as they left, he was overjoyed, and eagerly rushed to tell Molly, before returning to the waiting queue of farmers which stretched out of sight.

"Nay I ken it would be busy, but its nay always this bad, is it?"

"I warned you, didn't I?"

"Aye, but yon father dinna lose weight, like us, in this heat?"

Molly nodded again, as the autumn sun streamed into the mill, leaving them both drained. It was three weeks, before things slowed down, giving Molly a chance to get ready for the wedding. At their meal later, she couldn't contain herself.

"Dinah, said that Peg is bringing some food on the day, I`ve not met her or Maggie yet, but it's kind of them knowing I've no Mother to help me, isn't it?"

"Aye, but I wish wee William was coming."

"You'll all be together again, at Tom's wedding, next month won't you?"

"Aye, I'll have to wait till then."

When the harvest was over, the big day arrived and Molly sat at the window eager to see who came first.

85

"Peg's cart's here, with Bob and Dinah, and she's in her pretty blue bridesmaids dress, so she then can help me into mine."

The two of them hurried upstairs while Peg brought the food in, and Bob rushed up to his brother, with the matching shirts Betty on the market had made.

Harry and Maggie came next, with Tom and Alice in the back. Tom helped Alice down and carried some baking in from Maggie, before joining his brothers upstairs. Maggie carried in the cake and Harry brought his Elderberry wine. They joined Peg, and the three women filled the table up. There was much laughter and merriment coming from each bedroom, as they all dressed in their wedding attire.

The late October sun shone down, as if to bless their day. Tom, Dick and Alice left first, followed by Bob, who put Molly up at the front with him, and Dinah sat in the back on a clean cloth, so not to spoil her dress.

Harry, Maggie and Peg first checked the table and then they left in her cart.

At church Molly took Bob's arm, followed behind by an equally stunning Dinah.

"Aye, yee do make a bonnie bride Molly lassie, yon parents would be as proud as I am."

"That's lovely Bob, thank you for that."

Molly didn't want to cry, but the sight of all the other carts lined up outside the church, finally did it. She was astounded to see a packed church, filled with farmers and villagers all there for her. They were all used to seeing her in white in the mill, but they all gasped audibly as she passed. In her heavily crocheted, long sleeved, full length, elegant gown, that emphasized her voluptuous figure. Her long raven hair was flowing, just like it was the first time Dick saw her. She glided down the aisle in a dream, and wished that her father was there to see her. To her delight the ceremony went without a hitch and on the way down the aisle she whispered to her new husband.

"Dick, will you ask everyone to come back and share our wedding feast."

He complied, and everyone gathered at the mill, where the table was laden with home made pies, pastries, cakes and the magnificent wedding cake Maggie and Alice made. Peg had provided a varied assortment of cheeses, bread, butter and freshly boiled eggs, with lashings of milk. Harry's Elderberry wine added to it, there was plenty for everyone.

"I've never known such happiness; it's a day I'll never forget." Molly enthused.

"Aye and I'm the first brother to be wed; and soon it will be our Tom's turn."

The celebrations went on till dusk, by then all the farmers and villagers had long gone.

Peg left with Bob and Dinah, Molly thanked them all especially Dinah and Bob for the shirts and their support, which made their wedding day such a success.

Last to leave was Harry, Maggie with Tom and Alice in the back. Molly thanked them for everything they had done including the cake, and Dick thanked Tom, for being his best man. Before he left Harry gave him directions how to get to the wedding in November.

"See yee next month." They shouted and waved till they were out of sight, and then they breathed a sigh of relief. It had been a long exciting day, and they were exhausted as they shut the door.

"What a day, everything went well, and didn't Dinah look beautiful?"

"Aye she did, but nay as bonnie as yee, Molly lassie."

"Everyone's been so kind, Mother couldn't have done better had she lived. It's a shame Jim, didn't come, but I suppose someone's to milk the cows."

"Aye and I bet Bob and Dinah, were glad he dinna, he's been so nasty."

"I suppose so, but hadn't we better get all this mess tidied up?"

"Aye, we'll do it tomorrow, but now Mrs. Cardell, it's time we were away to bed."

Taking her hand gently, they went up to their room, which looked so different from when her father had slept there. They snuggled up for the first time, as tears ran down her face. "Yee're nay sad, about wedding me, are yee, Molly?"

"Never, I'm just being silly, take no notice."

"Silly, about what lassie?"

"About everything."

"Nay are yee worried, it's my first time too?"

"It's not just that, it's the mill."

"The Mill!"

"It's not the Hargreaves mill anymore; it'll be the Cardell mill."

"Aye but yee're a Cardell, Molly, and it'll always be called Hargreaves mill. I'll write the name on it if yee'll show me how, not that folks can read it." He laughed.

"I know that Hargreaves blood will run in our offspring's veins." She laughed too.

He kissed away her tears and erotically stroked her raven hair, exciting them both. Their lips locked, as their tongues sort out the innermost depths of their mouths. Their bodies writhing in unison, eager to explore their most intimate areas. All their inhibitions disappeared in the intensity of their emotions, carrying them to a higher level than either had ever anticipated. On that late October night, they became true lovers, and from then on, their lives would be complete. Honeymoons in those days were spent quietly at home. Dick and Molly were ecstatic after waiting for so long. That romantic time lasted only until the following

Sunday morning, when a cart pulled up outside the house.

Chapter 8 Bob

Bondswick market at the end of June kept Bob and Dinah very busy on their stall.

His life was then turned upside down yet again after meeting Tom and Alice on that late June evening. He was thrilled to hear that Dick was still alive and that he was to marry Molly the Miller after the harvest was finished. Dinah shared his joy and after packing up the stall that day they talked all the way home.

"Aye do yee ken the way to Cunningham mill, Dinah?"

"I'm sure we'll find it, after all Dick walked there after you parted, didn't he?"

"Aye, how far did I walk to Bondswick?"

"It doesn't matter, because we're going by cart."

"Nay I spent my time hiding in hedges, as the carts passed."

"I'm glad you came, you were brave coming dressed as you were."

"Aye, so am I, but I dinna feel very brave."

"You were in a strange country, just remember that."

"Aye, but if it wasna for Peg and yee, I'd have left to find Dick, because of Jim."

"Don't let him turn you away; Mum and I would really miss you."

"Nay, would yee miss me, Dinah lassie?"

"Yes, I would." She blushed.

He changed the subject feeling suddenly embarrassed.

"Aye it was grand seeing, Tom again and isna Alice lovely?"

"Suppose she is, if you like the sweet innocent kind?" She replied sharply

"She's nay as bonnie as yee, Dinah."

"Then I hope they'll be very happy, but what else did you talk about?" She leaned closer.

"He said Dick, it's odd but all our lives we've used our full names. I wonder if William's is shortened, he's nay a Will?"

"Do get on with it then!" She snapped.

"Aye Tom asked if we'd go and see Dick with us being so close, it'll be our first outing."

"I'll wear my best frock, shall I?"

He kissed her cheek as she cuddled up to him all the way home.

After he tended to the horse and cart, he returned to the house, where Jim's face was miserable again, but Peg beamed with delight.

"Dinah's told me your news and it's not before time too. So you'll be my son in law one day, and that's all right by me ...only I don't mean to rush things." She stammered and changed the subject. "I'm glad you've met Tom, Dinah says you'll see Dick on Sunday."

"When you wed our Dinah, go and live somewhere else." Jim grunted.

"Don't be stupid you silly boy, they'll have to live here." Peg chastised. "Or they won't be able get the cart ready, if they lived anywhere else will they?"

Bob was agog at Jim's suggestion and put it out of his mind for the moment. He was determined that he wouldn't spoil his joy at meeting Dick on Sunday.

It was Saturday morning and the last one of the week on the market; but Dinah felt a tension in him.

"You're quiet, Bob, have you gone off me?"

"Nay, but we should move if and when we get wed? Jim will only get worse after."

"I know, but we'll still have to run the stall, Mum can't do everything can she?"

"I dinna want to fret about that yet."

So they let things rest and Sunday could not come fast enough for him.

After breakfast they packed a picnic and dressed in their best clothes they left. It was a beautiful July day and Dinah showed him which direction to take. Bob had never been happier enjoying his day in the sunshine with Dinah by his side. They drove through parts of Lancashire that Bob had never seen before. Where quaint little villages were scattered about and all the cottages had thatched roofs and pretty gardens. On the village green the local men were dressed in white and were throwing a ball to a man who hit it with a bat.

"What are yon men doing, Dinah?"

She laughed and tried to explain how the game of cricket was played, but the more she said the more it confused him. His mind began to drift wondering what it would have been like if they'd all lived in a place like that, instead of living so far away from people.

"Aye it's grand around here; Dick must have thought so when he walked the same way."

Life was perfect for him now that he was settled again, if only Jim did not always spoil it.

"That's the Cunningham sign," Dinah exclaimed. "And look Bob, there's mill."

It took his breath away, seeing the black sails on a white mill shining in the sunshine. "Aye and what a grand place to live."

"I suppose it is, but I've never actually been here before."

A cart had just left as they pulled up to the mill, and Bob's heart beat wildly when he saw Dick, and who he assumed was Molly coming down the steps. He heard his own voice bellow out his name, and his brother shouted back. Dick then stumbled towards him and he ran from the cart to greet him. The formalities were soon dispensed with and Dinah took their picnic in with Molly to prepare their meal.

He and Dick never noticed how long the women were gone; as they were too busy finding out what had happened since they parted.

"Aye I'm glad we've met again, we've only to find wee William now."

"Aye but Tom's more likely to meet him, with going the same way?"

"Do yee nere think about what happened to us, afore the river that day?"

"Aye and I still have nightmares, but I've nay seen the river since."

"Aye we're lucky to have got through it, I hope wee William, did too."

At that moment the women brought in a fine spread of home cooked food, some Molly had made and a selection of Peg's produce, which they laid on the table. The conversation inevitably turned to their forthcoming wedding. Bob and Dinah were now included in it, and each had their separate duties to perform. Before they left Dick and Molly extracted a promise that they would return each Sunday, until the harvest time.

"Aye then we'll see yee next week?" Bob shouted as he and Dinah set off on that late bright summer evening.

"It was nice meeting Dick and Molly, and I'm glad we've been today."

"Aye we always got on, I'm glad yee and Molly do too."

"I've always wanted a sister, and we've both lost our fathers."

Snuggling up they drove on in high spirits, it was almost dark when they returned. Peg and Jim were in bed so Bob let Dinah go up while he unhitched the horse for the night.

The next six weeks continued like all the others until on the Saturday morning of the seventh week the sky was heavy with the prospect of a summer storm. By the time they set up the stall the heavens opened, so covers were thrown over their stock. Dinah, taking advantage of having no customers ran to see Betty. Scurrying back her head covered with a cape, she panted.

"It's all sorted and it's in my favourite colour, but this rain's getting worse."

"Aye I'd nay leave home in this, if I dinna have to."

He shivered, and his shoulder ached, as thunder and lightning flashed, and torrential rain lashed at the covers.

"Yee'd nay have expected this after yesterday, would yee?"

She nodded glumly as they got wetter than ever. The market was desolate as the storm continued and formed puddles in front of the stall, soaking their feet. It continued all morning and by midday all the stallholders had packed up and left.

"Aye, we should be away too, there's nay been a soul all day, has there?"

"Mum will go mad, she'd never come home early."

"Aye she would if nobody was about; let's be away we're wet through."

She reluctantly agreed, unconvinced that her mother would approve as they too packed up and headed home. The boxes were filled with rainwater as they carried them in to the dairy. Dinah went inside and he took a drenched horse for a rub down; but at the stable a rustling noise came from behind a pile of straw, he saw Jim in a state of undress with Nellie Parkinson from the piggery down the lane.

"Aye and what are yee doing?" Bob asked in dismay. "Peg might have found yee?"

"She thinks I'm milking, don't tell her?" Jim begged.

"Aye and yee Nellie should be away home." Bob urged.

"They're used to me going off, but we're in love, aren't we Jim?" She grinned.

"It's just a bit of fun Bob, its nowt to worry about." He squirmed.

"But yer said yer loved me Jim, or I'd not have kept doing it?" She wept.

Distressed by his words she ran out into the pouring rain her tears mingling with the large drops falling from the heavy black clouds. For the first time Bob had the upper hand.

"If yee dinna want Peg to ken, yee mun treat me better."

With a face like the thunder outside, he reluctantly agreed.

"Aye and afore yee go Jim, yee'd best take some milk back."

Glaring with vengeful eyes, he went to do just that.

With a sense of satisfaction he returned and saw Dinah crying and Peg looking severe.

"Nay, is this because we came home early, Peg?" He questioned.

"Dead right it is you'd have looked sick last winter if I'd packed up early wouldn't you?"

"Aye but yee only went once a week, and dinna think I'm nay grateful. Dinah and I go six days a week, so we mun make more money now. Everybody was away and there were nay customers. I'm sorry yee're upset, Peg, but dinna take it out on Dinah."

There was a deathly hush because he had never spoken to Peg like that before, but what he did say had made sense and she could not argue with it.

"So I flew off the handle and I'm sorry Dinah, you'd both better get changed or you'll have pneumonia? I'll make a hot drink for when you come down."

Walking up stairs Dinah beamed.

"Mum in full flow is scary, and I'm glad you told her."

After they came down Jim was standing by the fire smiling and surprised everyone. "Come and have a warm before you have your drinks."

Moving away he sat at the table and a strange silence followed.

"Am I in the right house?" Peg queried.

Dinah shrugged, each bewildered at Jim's change of heart.

"Whatever's happened, long may it continue." Peg said and then relaxed as they ate.

The atmosphere changed as Jim excused himself.

"I'm off to bed and I'll see you in the morning."

"Aye Jim, had a busy day?" Bob couldn't resist.

Jim's eyes flashed angrily as he slammed the door.

"I don't know what's happened, but it's been a long time coming." Peg said.

Bob did not explain, and things remained peaceful for the next couple of months.

Summer turned to autumn and the weather changed, making his shoulder ache.

Dinah picked up her bridesmaids dress from Betty and was delighted with it.

"Aye, will she make shirts for us? It'll be grand if we brothers looked smart too."

"I'll ask her, but what sizes shall I say?"

"Nay, Dick and I are the same, but, Tom needs a bigger one."

Next day Betty measured his neck and arm and he chose a colour like Dinah's dress. They had not been to the mill lately because it was harvest time; consequently Bob never had a chance to tell Dick what he had planned. Betty promised to get them done quickly and when they were made she had surpassed herself he thought. Bob hoped that Tom's was big enough. Even Peg had a dress made for the occasion. On their way home the day before the wedding Bob had a dreadful thought.

"I dinna get one for Jim and now it's too late."

"Don't fret, he won't come anyway."

"Aye, but it might start him off again."

"Mum would have said if he was coming."

"I canna believe it's only tomorrow, and wee William's nay there."

"Never mind, I'll go in while you see to things for tomorrow."

He prepared the cart for the journey and settled the horse, on his return he heard Jim talking.

"I'll stay and do the milking; you all have a good time."

His sly smile was just a bit too cheesy; and Bob wondered if he was still seeing Nellie. But he was only interested in the wedding and giving Molly away, to care what he did.

Early next morning they set off to be in good time, and none of them gave Jim another thought. The wedding went well and his brothers liked their shirts which did fit them. Giving Molly away was nay so bad he thought and they enjoyed the whole day, but left early to get home before dark. Jim was in bed when they arrived and had left a light on, but it was not long before they were all sound asleep.

Over the next week life returned to normal again, until the following Saturday evening. Dinah left him to see to the horse and the cart again, but when he returned there was shouting again coming from the house.

Inside Mr and Mrs Parkinson were yelling at Peg and she screamed even louder back. There was the now not so scrawny Nellie who wept and rubbed her swollen stomach. Jim hid behind Peg and denied everything, while Dinah listened in amazement.

"Jim's not to blame for Nellie; he never leaves me, except to do the milking."

As Bob arrived he was angry, that Jim refused to accept his responsibilities.

"Aye, so yee've been caught out, have yee?"

"Shut up, you've been nothing but trouble since you came!" Jim retorted angrily.

Her son's ferocious outburst, took Peg by surprise.

"You knew about this, Bob, and didn't tell me?"

"See Dad, I told yer he saw us!" Nellie screeched.

Bob was trapped between the warring families and looked for support from Dinah, to no avail. The Garner family united together leaving him isolated yet again.

"Aye" He admitted. "But its months since I found them, and he said it was all over."

"He's telling lies Mum, they all are?" Jim spluttered.

Peg was shocked and angry so she took it out on Bob.

"Shut up Jim! And as for you Bob, well, I wish you'd never come."

"Aye, well that's grand by me Peg; yee keep yon scheming son!"

Bob dashed upstairs to pack his few possessions; he was distraught that his life was once again shattered, as he heard the arguments continuing to rage downstairs.

"You should never have taken him in Mum." Jim ranted.

"That's enough Jim; you're in enough trouble as it is." Peg bellowed.

Dinah watched and listened and then realised that it was all Jim's fault as usual.

Bob in his room was devastated; because they were all supposed to be going to Tom's wedding in two weeks, and then he'd be seeing wee William. Granted he was guilty of blackmail, but it had made life better for a few months at least. A knock came on his door and it was Dinah with tears running down her face. He comforted her, kissing her long blonde hair afraid that his heart would break.

"You can't leave tonight, Bob it's too dark."

"Aye, I'm away to Dick`s, until I decide what to do."

"When Mum calms down, she'll ask you to stay."

"I dinna think so, but what's happening down there?"

"They're to be wed, but stay tonight and we'll go together tomorrow?"

He nodded, hoping that she would leave with him, so he stayed in his room.

But before he left in the morning Dinah was sitting at the table.

"Have some breakfast before you go Bob?" Peg asked.

Dinah glared at him to accept, but the atmosphere was strained.

"Aye and I'm sorry Peg, and thanks for taking me in, yee've been like a mother to me, but Jim's yon son and we'll nay get on."

Dinah fled heartbroken and even Peg's eyes were moist as she replied.

"I'm sorry too for blaming you, Bob, but don't go we need you."

"Nay, I hate to let yee down Peg, but I'm away to Dick and Molly's."

At that moment Jim came in from milking and his face was subdued, gone his cocky attitude, having to marry Nellie was punishment enough, Bob thought.

After breakfast, he and Dinah prepared to leave, when Peg ran out with her coat on.

"Will you drop me at the village Bob; I've to get the banns read for the wedding?"

"Aye, jump up Peg, I owe yee that."

There was an uncomfortable silence thinking that he was helping the pathetic Jim out. He only did it to repay Peg for her kindness and stopped at the church, to let her out. "Thanks, Bob, and I do hope that we meet again?"

"Aye, I'll see yee at Tom's wedding, that's if yee're still coming?"

"Dinah and I will be there, so we'll see you then."

"See yee soon Peg."

While continuing on to Cunningham they chatted.

"Don't let that so and so of a brother of mine spoil things for us, will you?"

Nay, it'll work out if Dick and Molly let me stay, but they've only just got wed. Dinna cry Dinah lassie, we'll see each other at Tom's wedding."

"But you'll go with them, so I'll have to see you there?" She sobbed

He nodded, barely able to speak the nearer he got to the mill.

"I'll miss seeing you everyday, Bob, don't stay away too long."

"Aye me too, but they might nay want me?"

"What, when you and Dick have always been so close, they'll let you stay."

He was unsure as they stopped at the mill, with his few possessions in the back of the cart and he wondered what kind of a reception he would get.

<u>Chapter 9 The Agreement</u>

Dinah nervously followed Bob into the house, to face his brother and Molly his wife.

"Aye there, I hope it's all right that we've come?" Bob said.

Dick and Molly, though surprised, replied together. "You are always welcome."

Bob reddened as he explained to both of them what had happened.

"Nay why, dinna yee tell Peg, when yee first found them?" Dick asked.

"Aye well, it gave me a chance to stop him from making my life hell." Bob admitted.

"Bob was so upset and he was going to walk here last night, I begged him to wait until we came today." Dinah defended him.

"Nay, so yee blackmailed him, did yee?" Dick frowned.

"Aye, and I'm paying for it, but I'll go if yee dinna want me to stay?"

"Nay, yee can stay here as long as yee like, canna he Molly?" Dick asked.

"Of course he can, I'll make up a bed in the spare room." She replied.

"Can I help you, Molly?" Dinah asked.

The women left the men to talk.

"Thank yee Dick and I'll help any way I can."

A crafty smile appeared on Dick`s face.

"Aye, yee'll earn yon keep all right Bob, there's something I want to do?"

"What's on yee mind?" Bob asked.

Dick explained his promise to Molly about writing the name Hargreaves on the mill.

"Nay do yee read and write then?" Bob gasped.

"Nay, and nobody else can, but Molly will show us what to do."

Bob laughed for the first time.

"Aye in that case, I'd best get my things out of the cart."

He soon returned with his few possessions and went up to see Molly and Dinah.

Later, the four of them shared a meat broth Molly had made the day before, and soon things returned to normal between them.

"Do yee promise to come next Sunday?" Bob asked.

Dinah nodded and drove off; he waved until she was out of sight and waited a while before going back inside.

"Nay, it'll be strange nay seeing Dinah, everyday."

"Aye, I'd feel the same if I dinna see Molly, to." Dick replied.

"Don't worry, Dinah, thinks you did right coming here." Molly comforted.

"Are yee sure Molly, I dinna want to spoilt yon honeymoon?"

"Our honeymoon will last all our lives, won't it Dick?"

"Aye it will, Molly." He nodded to her.

Their intimate smile made Bob feel embarrassed.

"I'm away to bed if we've a busy day tomorrow? Night, and thanks again."

"Aye, that's what a brother's for, Bob?" Dick said.

"Night Bob, will you be all right in Dick's old room?" Molly enquired.

"Aye, if it's good enough for him, it's good enough for me, Molly."

Bob was exhausted after his upset at Peg's, relieved to feel safe again at Dicks home.

Next morning he woke early as usual and was disorientated not being in his own bed. He heard Molly downstairs rattling around making breakfast and it smelt good. Eagerly he dressed and hurried down to join them, ready for what Dick had in store.

"Morning Bob, did you sleep well?"

Molly shouted from the kitchen while cooking their eggs and bacon.

"Aye, thanks Molly, but I miss seeing Dinah."

"Aye and I bet she missed yee too Bob, but dinna worry it'll all work out." Dick added.

After breakfast, Molly cleared the table and left them to get organised.

"Come on Bob, I'll show yee the mill afore we get started."

"Yee did well to ken how yon mill works Dick, but it's dirty at the front?"

"Aye, yee're right, we'll lime wash it."

"What with?"

"In yon barn there's daub brushes old Sam used, I'll show yee."

"They're dinna look long enough?" Bob questioned.

"Aye, then we'll cut some branches off yon trees, behind the mill."

They worked hard all day picking out the thickest to cut to the right length.

"Haven't you two started, yet?" Molly shouted.

"Aye, we've been cutting branches, to lime wash the mill." Bob explained.

"Let's hope the weather stays dry." Molly replied.

"We canna wait for better weather lassie, the mill gets busy then."

"Aye, and there's two of us so we'll get it done in nay time, canna we?"

"Nay, yee've some faith in me, Bob laddie."

"Aye, I always have had."

After dinner they went to the village for lime and black tar for the sails and stored them in the mill in case

104

it rained. It did as predicted, rain for the next two days, so it was Thursday before they could start at the base, which was the widest part.

"We'll share yon bucket Bob, yee do below it's better for yon shoulder and I'll work above, and get it done afore it rains again."

"Aye, but what about yon bad leg Dick?"

"Nay it'll be fine, dinna worry."

They used the daub brushes from the barn first.

"Aye it's grand working together, but dinna Molly mind me keeping yee apart?"

"Nay, it gives her a chance to bake and she dinna usually have the time."

"I feel bad letting Peg and Dinah down at Jim's wedding, but I canna go."

"Aye they'll ken that, yee're better away from him."

Later, Bob questioned.

"Do yee think on them back at yon croft?"

"Aye, everyday, they should have been at my wedding. But, we've got families of our own now; I only hope all is well back on Skye?"

"Nay mind Dick, we'll see wee William soon, and we'll all be together again."

"Aye, yee're right, Bob."

By Saturday three quarters of the base was done and luckily it had stayed dry.

"You're not doing any more are you? Dinah's coming tomorrow, not that you'll have forgotten, Bob?" Molly shouted.

"Aye, I've been counting yon days. We'll get cleaned up we've more lime on us than yon mill, I'm glad of a rest Dick; it'll take a fair time to do it all that's if it stays dry?"

"That's nay a problem, is it, Bob?"

"Nay but I've to find a job and a home for me and Dinah."

"Aye, I've told yee, it'll all work out, mark my words."

They washed in a bucket of water in the barn, rinsed the daub brushes and went in.

"Sit down; I've baked pork pies, if you can keep your eyes open?" Molly insisted.

"Aye, I could fair get used to this Molly, have yee enjoyed yon day?" Dick asked.

"I've washed the bedding and our clothes, cleaned the house and the baking, well it does itself didn't you know?"

They laughed, enjoying the easy banter together.

"Aye that pies grand Molly thanks, but I'm away to my bed, see yee in morning."

They answered in unison.

"Good night Bob, sleep well."

"It's nice having Bob, do you think things will be better with Dinah tomorrow?"

"Aye, but nere mind them; we'll have an early night, Mrs Cardell?"

"Certainly Mr Cardell, you're wish is my command." She giggled.

Bob left before breakfast to meet Dinah, jumping on the cart to greet her.

"Aye, I've missed yee lassie, how's it been this week?"

"It's not the same without you; we were rained off for two days." She grimaced.

"Nay, did Peg really, close the stall?" Bob gasped.

"We'd sold up, and Mum's, had things to do for Jim's wedding." She explained.

"Aye, let's forget about him lassie, guess what I've done this week?"

"Found a new job with a place for us to live?"

"Nay, we've started to lime the mill."

"How can you find a job, if you're doing that all day?" She scowled.

"Aye but I've to pay my way, just like yee do."

"You're right, I'm sorry, but will we ever be together?"

"Aye, Dick says something turns up when yee least expect it."

Arriving at the mill, he eagerly showed her what they'd done.

"It dinna look much, but we were rained off for two days too."

"Never mind that, come in Dinah I've been baking, while they've been doing the mill."

They followed her into the house and sat down to eat.

"How's things at home Dinah, is Jim's wedding arranged yet?" Molly asked.

"The banns are being read, and it's on the Monday before Tom and Alice's wedding. It'll be a quiet do Mum isn't having any drink, because the Parkinson's behave badly."

Bob frowned and Molly changed the subject.

"How's the weather been at the market?"

"It rained and we needed more stock, I don't know how long we can go on like this for?"

"Peg will have to do something, you won't be there forever." Molly said.

Dick interrupted.

"Aye, it'll be grand at Tom's wedding, I hope it dinna rain?"

"I canna wait for yee to meet wee William." Bob said.

"Why do you call him wee, is he so small, and who does he look like?" Dinah asked.

"Nay, it means he's the youngest and he's slimmer than us, so I'll have to watch yee."

107

"I wouldn't swap you Bob, even if we've to wait to be together."

"Aye well that's good, I'll get a job when the mills finished, and we'll wed." Bob said

"We'll get on with it Dinah, as long as the weather holds out." Dick added.

"I hope it does Dick, now I'm going to help Molly to wash up until it's time to leave."

Later, Dinah said her goodbyes before going.

"See you all next Sunday, and good luck finishing the mill."

Bob waved again till she was out of sight, before going to bed early again.

Monday was dry and they finished the lower level. Tuesday they reached the next level, before it rained solidly for the next four days, and Bob felt frustrated.

"Nay, I canna find a job and a home for me and Dinah, in this weather."

"Aye, I've told yee Bob, things will work out."

As usual on Sunday he again met Dinah, before breakfast.

"How've you gone on this week Bob? It rained us off for days."

"Aye, it stopped us too, and we've had nay farmers so I've nay found any work yet."

"Never mind, Harry and Maggie came to ask if I'd be Alice's bridesmaid."

"Nay, did yee tell them, I'm living here?"

"Mum told them about Jim, and that she's being a Granny too."

"Aye, but did they think we'd broken up, because I wasna there?"

"I said we meet each Sunday, and we'll all be at the wedding."

"Aye, that's good, now we'd best go or we'll be late again."

Everything went smoothly, and nobody mentioned Jim's wedding the following day.

Before Dinah left Dick reminded her.

"Aye, we'll meet by the river next Sunday after breakfast; Harry's told me the way so we'll go together?"

"Thanks Dick, Mum's taking Maggie to church because Harry's taking me and Alice. Do you mind if I wear the dress that I wore for yours Molly?"

"Why not Dinah, you looked beautiful in it, so I'll see you on Sunday."

This time all three of them waved her off.

Monday was dry but Bob was not fully concentrating, thinking about Jim's wedding. They used the cart to reach the top of the mill; Dick balanced on the side stretching over

"Be careful up there Dick, you don't look very safe?" Molly shouted.

As he turned, he lost his footing and fell heavily to the ground. She and Bob screamed his name together, each reaching him at the same time. His crumpled body lay motionless trapped between the cart and the mill, his leg and arm was crushed beneath him.

"Oh Bob! He's not …dead... is he?"

"Nay, but he hit his head on the way down and it's bleeding, get the doctor quickly?"

"I can't leave him, he needs me."

"I dinna know the way, hurry up and I'll carry him inside."

He straightened Dick's twisted and broken body, before struggling to carry him into the house. Afraid it was his fault for not seeing what might have happened, too concerned with his own thoughts. He placed him carefully onto the table, while he found a towel to wrap round his head to stop the bleeding. It was then that

Dick began to moan and Bob was relieved that he was still alive.

Molly soon returned with the doctor, who then examined him.

"Dick's broken leg has shattered knee bones in it and they've been there a long time. I'll remove them or his leg won't heal, his arm is broken on the same side. But they will heal given time; only it's his head injury that I'm worried about?"

Bob and Molly were afraid to say what had happened to Dick.

"He won't die, will he doctor, please say he'll live?" Molly begged.

Bob comforted her, and he was unsure who was shaking the most, and he would never forgive himself if his thoughtlessness had caused this to happen. He also knew that if it had happened on the croft Dick would have died for sure. They watched the doctor remove bits of bone from Dick's knee; it was that which caused him to limp for so long.

"He's very lucky, you did well to stop the bleeding, but he's in shock at the moment. Pass my bag young man."

Bob handed it to him and the doctor cleaned Dick's head with liquid from a bottle, before stitching it and then bandaging it up.

"Now I'll put some splints on his leg and arm, will you hold these for me young man so I can secure them firmly?"

Bob nodded, and he trembled keeping them in place, as the doctor tied twine at each end.

The pain made Dick react.

"Nay, leave me to die, yee go and see to the others!" Wild panic showed in his eyes and sweat poured from his brow. It reminded Bob of the battlefield when Dick was shot by a Redcoat's musket, amidst the noise and clamour of war. That was where hundreds of men were slaughtered, and their mutilated bodies were strewn all over the ground. He recalled the stench of death was rife, and the rivers ran red with their blood.

Fortunately Dick then passed out, but the doctor however became suspicious.

"What's he talking about, Molly? And who are these others he is on about?"

"Aye, we brothers loaded heavy stones onto a homemade cart back home and dragged it down the hill and it tipped over, Dick took the full force, that's what he meant." Bob lied.

The doctor grimaced.

"I thought there was some brain damage, will you give me a hand to get him into bed?"

Bob took Dick's shoulders being careful with his head, while the doctor secured his arm and took his legs. Molly in a trance led the way upstairs. They placed him gently onto the bed, leaving her to tend to his covers. While downstairs the doctor talked to Bob.

"Here are some herbs I've mixed, they'll help with the pain, he'll have quite a headache later. Will you be here to help Molly? I've known her since she was a baby, she is normally such a level headed young woman, but she's in shock just like you."

"Aye but we're away to a wedding on Sunday; it's the first time we brothers have been together for a year. Bob explained.

"He'd be better to rest and recover, but if you really must go, make sure that he's wrapped up warm and remains flat in the cart. I'll bring a crutch; it'll keep the weight off his leg until it heals."

"Aye, thanks doctor, what do we owe yee?" Bob asked.

"I'll sort it out with Molly, when I come back with the crutch."

111

When he left, Bob raced upstairs to see Molly holding Dick's good hand.

"Has he gone? What's he said? Is he going to be all right?"

"Aye, to it all! I was scared when he found yon injury, maybe Tom taking the musket ball out must have damaged the bone, so it's nay wonder he limped. The doctor's bringing something called a crutch, to keep the weight off his leg till it mends." Bob explained.

Dick began to come round.

"What's happening? It's my body that's hurt, nay my ears."

Molly laughed with relief that he was well enough to complain.

"The doctor said yee can go to the wedding, if yee stay flat on yon back in the cart. But yee must use this crutch thing and take this medicine. He took some bits of bone out of yon knee; but we dinna say how yee got the injury." Bob explained.

"I'm glad you dinna, I thought it was still on yon battlefield. My head aches and my leg and arm hurt too." Dick moaned.

Molly took the bottle off Bob.

"Take some of this, it's meant to help with the pain?"

Slowly the colour returned to his face, but Molly had furrowed lines on her forehead.

"Aye, I'll get washed and clean up, and I'll bring some water for Dick, will yee wash him Molly or shall I?"

"I'll do it Bob, but I don't know what I'd have done without you."

"Aye, but if I hadn't come, he'd nay have started the mill."

"It's not your fault; if I hadn't shouted then he wouldn't have fallen. Molly argued.

"Its nay body's fault it was an accident, and usually there's a reason for it." Dick retorted.

"We needn't go on Sunday, Tom and Alice will understand." Molly suggested.

"Nay go? I'm nay missing seeing wee William." Dick insisted.

Bob smiled and left them.

The doctor returned with a strange wooden contraption he called a crutch. He put it under his own arm, to show Dick how it worked and to make sure that he understood.

"You must use your good arm Dick, or your leg will never mend. I'll call to see you before you go, and I want to see you using it, remember."

"Aye, doctor I'll use it, I've to get better for Molly`s sake."

She went down to pay the bill, and then brought up bread and cheese, which they all ate.

"Aye it's a good job it happened today; I'll be fine by Sunday just yee see."

"Never mind about that, just get better to help me in the mill?" Molly chided.

"Nay slave driver, but I dinna ken how long it'll take." Dick joked.

"Bob will stay till you're well again, won't you? But it'll mean not getting a job or a place to live and it will keep you and Dinah apart."

"Aye, I'd nay leave Dick like this and I'll stay as long as yee need me. Dinah`s still to sort things out with Peg yet. Besides I've to finish liming yon mill yet."

"Thanks Bob, I knew you would, but don't worry about Dinah, things have a way of working out for the best, and you are my favourite brother in law." Molly added.

"Aye, that's because I'm the only one here Molly." Bob laughed.

Tuesday morning, Bob left Molly to fuss over Dick, while he carried on where they left off. It stayed dry and he finished the level they were up to, with great difficulty because of his shoulder. Dick had earlier stopped the sails turning before the accident, so that by Saturday a quarter of the top level was completed.

"Leave it now Bob, there's a lot to do before tomorrow. We've the cart to get ready for Dick, and it must be comfortable for him. I thought of bringing our bedding down, only if it rains, we'll need a cover to keep him dry."

"Aye, I'll do it now, is there anything else?"

"Yes, can you dress him in the morning and carry him downstairs, so we can both put him onto the cart." Molly added.

"Aye, is that all?"

"No, in your spare time, you can get yourself ready too."

They laughed, and he went to clean the cart ready for their early start.

Sunday morning, Bob took their bedding down and Molly made it up on the cart.

He then helped Dick to dress, before slowly and carefully getting him down the stairs. Molly toasted the bread with a fork over the fire, for breakfast. Later, they lifted Dick gently onto the cart and put his crutch and the pain mixture next to him.

They then set off very slowly, so as not to cause him any discomfort.

"Aye, Molly, come and sit up here next to me, so he'll rest and let the pain mixture work he might sleep all the way? It's going to be a long journey for him.

She reluctantly, agreed while constantly turning round to see if he was all right.

"Aye, I've always loved him, even when we were bairns." Bob explained.

Molly showed him the way to the river, and it was the first time he had seen it since they parted, and it still turned his stomach just thinking about it.

Peg and Dinah were waiting.

"Where's Dick?" Dinah enquired as Bob and Molly pulled up next to them. Peg too looked bemused.

"Aye he's in the back of the cart, and he's had a nasty fall." Bob said.

"But he was all right when I left last Sunday, so when did it happen?"

Molly couldn't speak, so Bob explained everything.

"Aye, but it happened on the Monday; he was standing on the side of the cart and stretched too far. His leg gave way; we thought he was dead, blood was everywhere."

"That was the day Jim and Nellie got wed, it was a bad for all of us. What a shock for you both, is he all right coming this far?"

"Aye I am, my body's a mess, but my ears still work." Dick shouted.

Dinah then walked round to see him.

"You look like you've been in a fight and lost." Dinah gasped.

"Aye and it feels like it too, but I've got this. He waved the bottle with his good arm,but his face was bruised even through the bandages.

Meanwhile, Peg chatted to Bob at the front of the cart.

"Are we are still friends? I miss you, and so does Dinah."

"Aye and I miss yee both, but I canna come back, Molly needs me more now."

115

"I understand, only it's not the same without you." Peg admitted.

Dinah joined Peg and waited for Bob to lead the way.

"Aye, Dick, which way did Harry say we've to turn, after the river?"

"There's wee a cottage at the end of the road, turn there." He shouted from the cart.

"We'll be behind you." Dinah smiled at Bob.

The convoy passed the cottage, where Tom was already waiting, sitting with William in his smart carriage and three ladies were sitting in the back.

Chapter 10 Tom

At Blackmoor Moss things were well underway preparing for Tom and Alice's marriage. She and Maggie were in the kitchen baking a wedding cake. Harry had warned Tom that things would get hectic once they returned home from the mill and he was right.

"You two had better get Alice's room ready; it needs a coat of whitewash? Tom, you'll have to sleep in the box room, so Alice can have yours while it's being done?"

"What did I tell you, Tom?" Harry shrugged.

Only he was not prepared for how fast Maggie's mind worked.

"Don't think you're getting away with anything Harry, you've the Elderberry wine to make for the guests? Our Alice can't fit into her dresses now, so I've to alter one of mine. When we do go to Bondswick we'll pick up a few things for the wedding, and we've to ask Dinah if she'll be our Alice's bridesmaid."

Tom's head spun. "Aye, but when are we doing the milking, and the deliveries, Harry?"

"It'll be hard, Tom, but we'll manage it."

Next morning, they left Tom with the milking while Alice made their breakfast.

"I'm glad Mum and Dad are out, I've missed our time alone."

Her glinting eye, made his heart race.

"Aye, but what about the bairn, lassie?"

"The baby won't mind, so after breakfast let's make the most of it?"

Tired as he was, he eagerly finished his meal.

Later, as they lay on the bed exhausted after their frenetic lovemaking, they chatted. "Aye, lassie will that do yee till we wed?"

"It's ok, I suppose!" She smiled seductively at him, and they spent all day in bed.

"Now, we've really christened our new bedroom in style, haven't we?"

"Aye yee are a wicked lassie Alice." He grinned. "Nay that I mind, but dinna yee think we'd best be away down, they'll be back soon?"

"Spoilsport, but you're right." She pouted.

They were down just as the cart drew up outside, Maggie rushed in with two parcels, while Harry saw to Daisy and the cart.

"Come see what I've got Alice, there's one each for us to wear next Sunday."

Opening each parcel Maggie produced two bonnets in different colours.

"We'll look like gentry, thanks Mum, but did Dinah say she'd be my bridesmaid?" "Yes, but she'll wear the same dress she wore at Dick and Molly's wedding."

"It won't matter; I'll look huge next to her by then anyway."

"Aye, but yee'll make a bonnie bride, how ever big yee are." Tom argued.

"I'm glad we don't have weddings every month." Harry moaned as he entered.

"Aye but dinna Dick and Molly's wedding go well." Tom mentioned, trying to ease Maggie's stress about theirs. "So Maggie the food was grand then and it'll be the same for us, it always is?"

"I know all that Tom and I thought your two brothers were fine young men, and that Molly and Dinah were lovely young women too. It's a day I'll never forget and that's why I want yours and our Alice's to go as well as theirs did."

118

"Your wasting your breath Tom lad, she can't help but to worry, it's in her nature."

"Don't think you've both finished yet? This house needs a good clean, I'm, not being shown up in front of everyone."

"Told you what it would be like, didn't I?" Harry shrugged.

"Aye, but we canna leave it all to her Harry? She just wants our wedding to be grand."

"Then we'd best get some rest, it'll be our last chance for a while."

After breakfast when the milking was done and it was kitted in the churns he and Harry set off, but it was afternoon when they returned.

"Here goes, hang on to your hat, she'll have our orders ready." Harry joked.

"Aye," Tom shrugged. "Let's get it done; we mun help her Harry."

It was a hectic time at the farm, and the preparations for the wedding were going well. But it still didn't stop Maggie from worrying and finding more things for them to do.

"She'll have us scrubbing the yard next or want the cows washing too." Harry moaned.

"Nay she'll nere do that, will she?" Tom asked.

"It wouldn't surprise me if she didn't want the barn tidying up too." Harry continued.

"Come off it Harry, she'll nay go that far, will she?"

As they returned to the house Maggie had started again and poor Alice looked worn out.

"Is everyone coming here? Or are we meeting them all at church? Will your William, know where to come?"

"Stop fussing woman, I told Dick the way and it'll depend what time they get here, besides, William can read the signs to the farm."

119

"I know he's Tom's best man, but how do we all get to church?" Maggie persisted. Dinah, is Alice's bridesmaid, so who goes with who?"

"Stop fretting woman, there's four carts so we'll sort it out, when everyone comes." "You don't think about anything, how's old Alf and Queeny getting there?"

"One of the lads that help at the harvest will pick them up." Harry sighed.

"But how many are coming? Is there enough food for everyone?"

"Aye, there's always enough food Maggie, yee've to enjoy yon wedding too."

"You're a nice man, Tom and I'm glad our Alice is marrying you. Oh! I'm supposed to be seeing how her dress fits; she'll be waiting upstairs for me."

Tom recalled the words Maggie had said when they told her they were having a bairn; it was only then it struck him like a thunderbolt, that this is what his father had meant.

"Nay is everyone's wedding like this, Harry? Dick and Molly's was all right."

"That's because there was no Mother hen fussing over her, Maggie's Mother was just the same at our wedding."

"Aye and is that why yee wanted to keep away? I'm glad it only happens once, but I'm still afeard about Alice."

"Why? She loves you, and you love her, don't you?"

"Aye, but her having the bairn, worries me." He immediately regretted saying it.

"Our Alice is young and healthy, and besides Maggie won't leave her."

"Aye I ken that, and I'm glad she is, and that the doctor's in yon village."

"Come on let's get this hay delivered and get out of here?" Harry changed the subject

"Aye, I'll be glad when it's over, but it'll be grand us brothers being together again."

He was glad Harry didn't know his guilty secrets, but now Dick was wed, it would only cause trouble if he knew the truth.

"Our Maggie will be fine by the wedding Tom, and she'll enjoy it then."

"Aye I ken that, but in less than a year two of us brothers will be wed?"

"You've done well for yourselves, your parents would be proud."

Tom was not so sure, as his father took the truth with him to his grave.

"Yee ken I love it here Harry; the cows always need milking, and even in winter I dinna mind turning them into yon yard, while the cowshed is sluiced."

"I knew you were the man for me the first day we met, and I'm glad everything is ready for the wedding next week. But I could do without trailing to Bondswick tomorrow; and goodness knows what else Maggie wants this time."

Next morning, they left early, and after milking Tom returned to the house. He was relieved that Alice was too tired to make love this time; as he wanted to talk to her.

"Aye and will we still live here after the bairn comes, Alice?"

"Why, where else can we go?" She gasped.

"I dinna ken, but it will all change after it's born, won't it?"

"Change, in what way?"

"Maggie will take over when it comes; she'll nay be able to stop herself will she?"

121

"But, I don't know what to do with a baby, so I'll need her help, Tom."

"Aye, but it's our bairn Alice lassie and we should raise it."

"Are you saying, that we should leave the farm, Tom?"

"Aye, we'd rent somewhere close, but I'd still work here."

"So, you'll be out all day and leave me alone, with a new baby by myself?"

"But I'll nay have much to do with it, if we stay here, will I?"

"Of course you will, it'll sleep in our bedroom."

"Yee dinna ken, I cared for my brothers and sisters each time Mother had another bairn. That's why I want to care for our own bairn."

"Oh, Tom, I never thought, but I'll need Mother's help, as I don't know what to do."

"Aye I see, Alice lassie, only dinna leave me out, will yee?"

"I'd never do that Tom; you'll see it each time you eat."

"Aye, we'll see, so long as I get to spend time with it. I ken that your parents will be happy, with it being their first grandbairn."

"I'm glad we've talked, Tom, so let's think about names for our baby."

"Aye, what do yee like, Alice?"

"If it's a boy, I'd like to call it Henry as its Dad's real name, and Margaret if it's a girl after Mum, what do you think?"

"There yee are, it's all yon family, what about mine?"

"I'm sorry Tom, you think of a name."

"The first son is always called Thomas, and the first girl is Jennet, my sister was called Jinni."

"What shall we do, then?"

"If it's a laddie we'll call him, Thomas Henry, but use Tommy, if it's a lassie Jennet Margaret, or Jenny, if you like?"

"That will please both of us, and if we have more children, we can change the names round, will that do?"

"Aye and just how many bairns, are we're going to have, Alice?"

"I'm not having an only child, it always sounds good having brothers and sisters."

He was afraid to say that she might die having this baby, instead he answered.

"I dinna say it was grand, we dinna have much as bairns."

"But, you had each other and that's something I'd have liked."

"Aye, well if we're having so many, we canna stay here then, can we?"

"I think by then, Mum and Dad would be glad, if we did go." She laughed.

They enjoyed the remainder of the day, sharing their meals and making plans, and were completely at ease with each other. Tom wished it could always be like that.

He was fond of Maggie she was always nice to him and he had a great respect for Harry. His only problem was that he was still only a lodger in the house, which might change when he and Alice get wed. Time just seem to fly and they heard the cart pull up outside.

Maggie rushed in again and this time her arms were full of parcels.

"I've lots to tell you Tom; do put the kettle on, Alice?"

"Aye and what's happened?"

Taking a deep breath, she began.

"Jim married Nelly from the pig farm yesterday, and now Peg's going to be a granny just like me. Bob found them once and Peg was angry and told him to go. Only now she's sorry, and wants to make it up again on Sunday."

"Nay have they broken up?" Tom gasped.

"No, Dinah took him to Cunningham and she sees him on Sundays, he's helping Dick to lime wash the mill."

"Aye, so what about yon wedding, are they all still coming?" Tom asked.

"Peg and Dinah are meeting them by the river and they will follow them here."

"Aye, I hope it's sorted afore that, I dinna want it to spoil seeing William again."

"They love each other and want a place of their own Dinah said." Maggie added.

Alice then returned from the kitchen.

"Here's your drink Mum and I've made Dad one too."

Harry then walked in.

"What a good lass I'm parched, has your Mum told you the news?"

"Yes I heard it, poor Dinah, she must be so upset."

"Nay, its poor Bob, and now he's to start all over again, hasna he?" Tom responded.

Harry knew they would be upset and quickly changed the subject.

"Have you shown them your new things yet, or are you too busy gossiping?"

"I was... only just saying... Bob's all right with Dick and Molly."

"They'll sort things out on Sunday, now show them what you've got."

"Sounds good, come on Mum let's see." Alice brightened.

Unpacking her parcels Maggie explained.

"I've got us both new shawls in case it's cold, yours will match your dress, and I hope you like it?"

"Thanks Mum they're lovely, now we'll look like royalty." She beamed.

"Glad you like it, Dinah said you would, Betty on the market knitted them. I didn't forget you men either; I hope it fits Tom, Harry's does?"

"Thank yee, Maggie, but I'd have worn the shirt I had for Dick`s wedding, but now Harry and me will really look the part."

"You know our Maggie, she always gets it right, and they'll do for Christmas."

"Christmas is a special this time and it's Alice and Tom's first one wed." Maggie said.

"You're right Mum, but next year there'll be another one to share it with us."

She gently patted her bulging tummy, and Tom hoped that she was right.

"I hope it doesn't rain on Sunday or we'll all get wet. Maggie mentioned

"What if does Dad; we'll all be soaked through?" Alice panicked and worry lines appeared again on her pretty face.

"How do you think we farmers go on, lass? We've covers to keep the grain and hay dry so we'll use them. We'll do anything, to protect you on your wedding day lass. Come on Tom, we'll give them a scrub just in case. The guests will have to do the same; but we'll make it a day to remember, for you lass."

"I hope so, but what if you need them before Sunday?" Alice questioned.

"Then, we'll clean them again, we'll not be long."

"Nay Alice lassie in summer it rains, yee leave it to us."

"You're right, Tom, I'm only being silly, take no heed of me."

"If it puts your mind at rest lass, me and your groom will do anything."

Leaving the women to get on with their chores, they scrubbed the covers in the barn, while planning another surprise for Alice. The weather was atrocious for the next few days, throwing Alice into a flap again. Maggie kept her busy in the kitchen.

"It's a shame Aunt Bessie and Uncle Ted, can't come, isn't it Mum?"

"The only folks coming are those we've asked, we can't tell them at Eastrick, unless you've got a carrier pigeon somewhere?"

"If I had, I'd send it to Skye, and get Tom's family here."

"That's a nice thought Alice, but we'll make do with the family he's got, there'll be enough with those they're bringing with them won't there?"

Alice looked out at the rain. "Tom and Dad will be drenched; I hope it stops before Sunday. His brothers will be too, coming such a long way in this weather, won't they? I'm getting excited; do you think Molly felt like this? It's sad she hasn't got a mother like me."

"She'll have missed her father too; I bet she'd have liked him to give her away instead of Bob."

Tom and Harry arrived back and shook the rain off their clothes.

"If it's like this on Sunday Alice lass, you'll be dry till we get to the church, it's only when we get home you might get wet, so you'll be dropped off at the door."

"Thanks Dad, come and get dry both of you. I'll make a warm drink."

"Something smells good, is it for tea?" Harry sniffed. "It's damn cold out there today."

126

"It's all for the wedding, but there's pork pie and potatoes for tea."

"By that sounds good, if it's like this at Dick`s, it'll stop the liming being done."

"Aye, and Dinah and Peg will be soaked too; everyone suffers when it's like this. Will it be raining for William, in Freestone, do yee think?"

Maggie then breezed in. "Teas ready! So enjoy it while it's hot, our Alice has been a big help today, and I'm glad you'll be staying with us Tom."

He almost choked on his food.

It had rained non stop even on Saturday, while Tom and Harry delivered two days milk to their customers.

After dinner Maggie and Alice washed up and got the wooden bath in and boiled the water from the well in a pot over the fire while Tom and Harry went outside to prepare Alice's surprise in the stable.

"I'll scrub the cart and we'll put a clean cover on, for whoever rides in the back? Will you cut some Holly, to decorate it with and then use strong branches off the apple tree to tie on the top? It'll have to cover me, Alice, and Dinah in the back? I suppose you'll come back with the bride?"

"Aye, Dinah will come back with Bob, but if it's wet we'll all fit in together."

Harry cleaned the wheels while Tom fixed the branches and twisted the foliage.

"Aye, is yon strong enough Harry?"

"That'll do fine, Tom, we don't want the wheels jamming up. I've some twine on that shelf behind you, as the winds very strong this time of year."

After it was finished, they looked at Daisy.

"She'll need grooming, and we can tie ribbons on her tail, that's if she keeps still."

"Aye, Harry yee've been like a father to me, and thanks for letting me wed Alice."

Harry patted Tom's shoulder.

"I'm glad the wheel came off that day, or we'd not have met, appen it was just fate."

They hugged each other, the way he hugged his brothers almost a year before.

"Our Alice will be surprised, now we'd best get scrubbed up for the big day, Son."

Tom smiled, because soon he would really be his son in law, and went in for their baths.

"What have you two been doing for so long? We've have had our baths and the tubs ready for you two now. Our Alice went up for an early night, she couldn't keep her eyes open, but she sends her love Tom and says she'll see you at the church tomorrow."

"Canna I see her in the morning, Maggie?"

"It's unlucky for the bride to see the groom, before the wedding." She insisted.

"Aye, but we live in the same house, it dinna seem right?"

"Don't try to understand women Tom, they've got strange ideas."

"Aye if she's upstairs, I'll get ready and be away for a walk if it dinna rain." He said.

"I'm all right being here, as I'll be giving her away, aren't I?"

"Yes of course Harry, let's hope its dry tomorrow, so that Tom can leave."

His face fell.

"Aye, I'll walk to the crossroads in case wee William comes first, I ken Martha, but I've nay met Emily or Ruth yet. Who lives the nearest, do yee ken Harry?"

"I don't know where Freestone is, but it's about as far as Bondswick is to Cunningham.

It'll depend what time they all leave. They could all get there at the same time, so you'll get a lift back from any of them, won't you?"

Maggie handed them their plates.

"I've kept your meal warm, I'm off to bed we've a big day ahead of us, haven't we?"

"Aye, night Maggie, and thanks for all yee've done, if I dinna remember tomorrow."

"Night Son, it's been a busy day, and soon you'll really be one of the family."

A shiver ran down his spine having a new set of parents after all these years. All he had to do now was deal with the guilt he had carried for so long. Tomorrow his life would change forever and he'd never be alone again, so long as Alice was safe.

Tom spent an unsettled night and in the morning it was dry. He dressed in his best black britches and shoes and put on his new shirt before going downstairs. Maggie and Harry waited to have their wedding breakfast with him; afterwards he got up to leave.

"Aye I'll be away to meet them, and thanks again, I'll see yee at the Kirk. I'll come back with William, and yee can meet them all later, we'll wait for the others afore we go."

"Thanks Son, our Alice is a lucky girl having such a caring man, at the Kirk."

Maggie laughed at his word for it and he blushed; he had tried so hard to speak English.

"Aye I'm away now Maggie, and thanks, see yee later Harry and drive my bride safely."

He turned sharply so they did not see a tear in his eyes as he set off to meet his brothers.

Tom waited by Queeny Carter's gate, and Williams's carriage came first with the Bradmans in the back and Emily up front, he grinned and frantically waved to them.

Chapter 11 The Reunion

As Williams's carriage drew up outside Queeny Carter's cottage, Tom was glad that he had arrived first. So that he could spend time with him and his new family, before the others arrived.

"Dinna expect yee to be here, Tom?" William greeted him.

"Aye, I'd to be away so Alice can get ready; it's nay fair, so I came to meet yee all."

They laughed and William took him straight over to the carriage to meet Emily and Ruth.

"Tom do come and meet my wife Emily."

"Aye, but I dinna ken about that." Tom asked as he thrust out his hand. "It's grand to meet yee Emily and that yee are a Cardell now."

"Thank you and I am pleased to meet you too Tom" She shook his firm hand. "I have heard so much about you; and we were married on the same day as Dick and Molly."

"Nay, it's a shame I wasna there."

"Aye, it was only because Emily's father was away to a parish in Eastrick."

"That was not the only reason though William, we do love each other too."

"Aye, I'm sorry lassie, but I'd told Tom, we were only courting then."

"Nay matter, I'm happy for yee; but did yee say yon father went to Eastrick, Emily?"

"Yes Tom, but why do you ask?"

"Harry's sister Bessie and her husband Ted live there, he told people I was his nephew to cover up that I was a Jacobite."

"How very strange, I wonder if they will ever meet. But how was it at Dick and Molly`s wedding?" Emily asked.

"Aye, her face was bonnie seeing the Kirk full of people who came to see her,"

"It sounds just how a wedding should be. Ours was to be a quiet affair, Martha and one of my pupils were my bridesmaids."

A jovial voice then shouted from the back of the carriage.

"Hello there again, Tom."

He walked round the carriage to speak to her.

"Aye there Martha, grand to see yee again, and this must be Ruth?"

"I'm pleased to meet you, Tom, and thanks for asking us.

We don't go to many weddings, but this will be the second in a month."

"Ruth was my best woman," William explained. "And Emily's father married us, and our Kirk was full of folks all there to wish us and him well."

"Aye and I'm glad yee had a grand day, I hope mine turns out as well."

"It'll be special," William smiled. "As we'll all be together again, won't we?"

"Aye and three of us will be wed in less than a year, there's only Bob's left then."

"A good job its dry Tom," Martha laughed. "Or you'd be wet through waiting there."

"I dinna know if any of yee ken the way to the Kirk?"

"Will yee come back with us Tom?" William enquired.

"Aye, but canna we wait for the others to come?"

"Aye, if yon ladies dinna mind?"

All three nodded, and then Emily suggested.

131

"Tom do come and sit next to William, I will join Ruth and Martha."

"Will yee have enough room back yonder?"

The sisters answered in unison.

"Don't you worry about us Tom, we'll be just fine."

"Aye and what are yee up to now William?" Tom asked.

He explained everything and that Emily ran a school so the children can read and write.

"Nay what's this world coming to when bairns can read? If we'd ken how to, we'd have ken where we all were. Harry taught me numbers to count sacks of grain and pay for them. Dick and Bob ken theirs too, but we canna read."

"Aye, now it's an idea Emily lassie," William said. "Teach yon parents canna yee?"

"I had not considered it before, but what a very good idea: I could teach them in the evening after their work. Thank you for suggesting it Tom, what a pity we are not nearer, or I could teach you all."

Tom liked Emily, but then he noticed Ruth's eyes were glinting at him.

"William said I'd love you, and I can't wait to meet his other two brothers."

Tom flushed and thanked her adding that he was glad that she had come today.

"Do all your brothers have beards like you, Tom?" Ruth asked.

Embarrassed he shook his head, and it was then a rumble of wagons was heard.

"Aye, they're here, I canna wait to see them again." William beamed.

"Yee dinna ken it but Bob's staying at Dick and Molly's," Tom explained. "Dinah's brother caused some trouble and he left three weeks back."

"Are they still together?" William asked.

"Aye and Dinah goes on Sundays," Tom nodded. "He and Dick are liming the mill."

"Who's that yon, sitting next to Bob?" William asked.

"It's Molly," Tom replied. "But where's Dick? "We'll soon we'll find out."

"Hey there Bob," William shouted. "Grand to see yee again, but where's Dick?"

"Aye there William," Bob replied. "We canna wait to see yee, but Dick`s injured."

"I'm Molly, your sister in law; it's nice to meet you at last William. Dick didn't want to miss you, so he's in the back of the cart."

"I'm hurt woman not deaf or dumb," Dick shouted. "So let me see wee William."

He and Tom went round and were aghast to see him.

"What have yee done?" William enquired.

Dick told them all that he could remember and then Bob and Molly finished it off.

"Is it yon bad leg that's hurt, Dick?" William asked.

"Aye, the doctor found bits of bones," Dick said. "He said it's why I limped."

"Nay it's all my fault taking yon shot out of it." Tom flushed. "Yee should rest at yon farm instead of coming to the Kirk."

"I'm away to see you wed Tom," Dick waved the bottle. "I've got this for the pain."

William explained they were married on the same day and he had thought about him.

"Aye we could have had a double wedding," Dick joked. "If only we'd ken about it."

Peg's cart then pulled up beside them, and all the introductions took place.

"I've heard about you William, I'm Alice's bridesmaid, and you're Tom's best man?"

"Aye and we both have jobs to do today."

133

Time was getting on and Tom began to fret.

"Follow us," He said and joined William in the carriage leading the convoy to the farm and the ladies listened as they went.

"Bob'll be away at the mill till Dick`s better," William said. "And it'll be some time. He's lucky yon fall dinna kill him, and wee Molly`s only been wed as long as us. I'm afeard to think how Emily would feel, if it was me."

"I dare not think about it William," Emily interrupted. "I must speak to Molly later."

"We'll all meet when we get to the Kirk." Tom assured her.

"I bet yee dinna expect all this, when yee arranged our reunion? "William said. "We nay suffered such injuries, fighting the English last year, did we?"

"Yeer right," Tom nodded. "We're lucky to have got away with our lives apart from our injuries, but accidents happen anywhere dinna they? Here is the farm; I'll just show Dinah where to put the cart."

He got down to sort things out, giving William, a chance to talk to his wife.

"So this is where Tom ended up." William said.

"You two certainly travelled a long way from each other." Emily added. "But it is good that you are all together again."

"Nay," He sighed. "Those at Skye canna be here."

"In time there will be a way to contact them." Emily consoled him. "My father as well."

"It'd nay be much good," He shrugged. "They canna read or write."

"Things will change," Emily persisted. "One day everyone will read and write."

"It'll nay be in my lifetime for sure," William grimaced. "Aye I hope yon right anyway."

134

Tom then shouted from the farm entrance and disturbed their conversation.

"Pull forward William, Dinah canna get the cart in."

"We'll be away down the lane a wee bit." William responded.

Tom soon retuned red faced to join them.

"Aye it be all sorted; now let's be away to the Kirk."

"Why have yee a cheeky smile on yon face, Tom?" William asked.

"Yee wait and see?" Tom shrugged. "When Alice arrives at the Kirk."

"It all sounds very mysterious Tom?" Emily questioned. "What have you done?"

"We've done things special for Alice," He grinned. "Yee will soon see."

"Isn't it exciting?" Ruth exclaimed. "Old spinsters like us, enjoying ourselves."

"You speak for yourself," Martha reacted. "Just remember your older than me."

They all laughed as they arrived at Saint Ann's Church in Blackmoor village. William dropped off the ladies, and moved his carriage to let Bob and Molly's cart through.

Then the three brothers struggled hard to get their injured and persistently moaning brother into church. Molly watched with a worried expression on her face as the ladies approached, and Emily introduced everyone.

"I'm pleased to meet you all," Molly replied. "But I'm worried about Dick."

Emily and the Bradmans comforted her, and as she stumbled Emily caught her.

"I'm sorry," She apologised. I don't know what's wrong with me, I feel so weak."

"You are in shock," Emily said. "I bet you have not slept since the accident?"

"Your right," Molly nodded. "I daren't shut my eyes in case Dick needs me."

"Can nobody help?" Ruth asked. "It must be a strain running the mill as well?"

"I'm an only child Ruth, and I don't know what I'd have done without, Bob."

"Why not ask Dinah to stay?" Emily suggested. "I am sure she would gladly help. It might also solve Bob's problem, of not seeing her."

"I'd love her to come," Molly brightened. "And Bob would be pleased too."

Their conversation ended abruptly, as the wedding cart's arrived and they all scurried into church and took their appropriate seats.

Inside Tom never noticed the rows of people watching him from the back of the church, because he was listening to Bob and Dick talking.

"Here it only leaves thee Bob to get wed now." Dick grinned.

"It canna be for ages," He replied. "Dinah thinks Peg still needs her on the stall."

Tom turned on hearing this.

"Peg ran it alone, when yee first met her last year, dinna she?"

"Aye Tom, but then Dinah and Jim made everything she needed."

"Why dinna Jim and his wife do it?" Dick suggested. "What do yee think wee William?"

"I'd sort things out while they're both here." He replied. "Just speak to her later."

"Yee are right, I'll do that." Bob replied brightly.

Dick then saw the women come into the Church.

"Here's they are, I bet they've been gassing outside."

"You mean, just like we've been doing?" William joked.

"Less cheek wee William" Dick rebuked. "I'm injured, but I'll still sort yee out."

"Come on then let's see yee try" He laughed. "But I'm nay wee William anymore."

"Sorry," Dick flushed. "It's just something I've always said, I dinna mean nay harm." "Dinna fall out," Tom said. "It's the first time we've been together for nigh on a year." "Sorry," Dick apologised. "I dinna want to spoil yon wedding more than I have already."

A sudden disturbance from the back of the church halted the conversation, and it started Tom's nerves jangling.

"Someone's here, come on William, we'd best get to our places."

Tom was glad to see Queeny and old Alf sitting on Alice's side of the church, along with the farm hands that helped during the harvest. He held no animosity to them anymore as it was he who was marrying Alice today. It would please Alice though that so many people had come to see them get wed, he thought.

Standing at the altar rails with his brothers sitting behind him, Tom wished that Jinni, John and Ellen were there too. He saw Maggie and Peg arrive both looking very smart in their Sunday best. They smiled before sitting in the front pew on the opposite side.

His heart then began to race, knowing Alice was next on the arm of a very proud Harry. He knew that Bob's eyes were only for Dinah looking so beautiful, following on behind.

Tom's head spun and panic overtook him, could he say his vows in front of everyone?

He wanted to marry Alice, but the occasion overwhelmed him. His hands were clammy as his sweating fingers fiddled with the collar of his new shirt. He noticed Dick and Bob were wearing the matching shirts, they had for his wedding. As for William, if he had turned up in his working clothes he would look smart. Tom realised that everyone's eyes would be on Alice, but it did not calm his nerves.

He felt an awkward hulk of a man standing next to his slim and handsome youngest brother. His mouth was dry and he found it difficult to swallow. The last time he felt like this, was when the Laird's men took them from their home. Yet here he was with his brothers and everyone who cared about him, waiting for Alice to marry him. So why did he feel so scared on this, the greatest day of his life? He wondered if William and Dick felt like that on their wedding day. The only difference between them was that their wives were not having a baby at the time. They also did not carry any guilt about their own mother's death and none of them knew how he felt, as his knees began to buckle. For an awful moment he thought he was going to pass out. He was the eldest, who always sorted everything out, only now he must pull himself together before he made a complete fool of himself. This much anticipated reunion did not turn out to be what he expected. William was married, Dick was battered and bruised, and Bob was apart from Dinah.

While he carried this dreadful guilt, so why could he not let it rest, would he ever be free of it? His mind was in turmoil.

"Yee all right, Tom?" William enquired. "Only yee look a bit queasy."

"Me, I'm grand." He gulped. "It's just the waiting that gets me down."

"I felt the same so dinna worry," William comforted him. "Alice will be here soon."

He loved William for his common sense approach to life, and envied that about him. "Yee're right, I'm so glad that yee are here, and I'm sorry I wasna there for yee?"

"Oh yee were there in my heart," William smiled. "So were the rest of my family."

A lump came in his throat, like the one when they parted almost a year ago. He then realised whatever worries he had, he was lucky to have three brothers with him today.

Chapter 12 Tom's wedding

Tom was right, as the buzz of excitement reverberated around the church. His knees began to tremble yet again, but a wink from William, put him at ease. Alice looked a picture in her long pink poplin gown, with a white lawn frill round the neck. Maggie did a good job letting out the pink braided bodice, to allow it to fit her. Fortunately she wore the shawl that Maggie bought her and it concealed everything. Seeing her pretty face made all his previous inhibitions disappear, except for the one concerning her safety having the baby. Immediately as she reached him the organ stopped and the minister began the service.

"Dearly beloved, we are gathered here today…"

Tom heard the words, but could not believe it was actually happening; it was a nudge from William that brought him back.

"Do you Thomas; take Alice, to be your lawful wedded wife?"

They had rehearsed this together so many times and he only had two words to say.

His mouth went dry again and he could hardly swallow, there was a prolonged silence until he controlled himself and answered. "I do."

The sigh of relief was audible and showed on Alice's face. After this stumble the ceremony then continued without a hitch, as the minister concluded.

"I now pronounce you man and wife, you may kiss the bride."

He did, and the congregation clapped making him blush.

"You scared me," Alice whispered. "I thought you'd changed your mind."

"Nere!" He smiled. "I canna speak, yee took my breath away, but yee always did."

"What a lovely thing to say," She blushed. "And by the way thank you for the beautiful cart, I can't wait for everyone to see it. Daisy hated wearing a ribbon so Dad took it off." "I love yee Alice Cardell," Tom beamed. "So let's be away home I'm starving."

She linked his arm and he proudly led her down the aisle, and then he noticed Harry talking to Queeny, Alf and the farm lads, he knew then that they would all come back.

The cart was ready outside and he helped his new bride up in her mother's wedding dress, which only the four of them knew about.

"Will Dick be all right?" Alice asked. "Dinah, told me what happened, she's so upset."

"William and Bob will help him on the cart," He explained. "Aye Dick's tough to come all this way like that."

"I hope Bob and Dinah can sort things out," She continued. "If Peg doesn't spoil it." "Me too," He agreed. "Are Maggie and Harry coming back with us?"

"No," She shook her head. "Peg's bringing them with Dinah, so it's just us two."

He smirked with delight.

"I canna wait for to yee to meet William, Emily and the Bradmans."

"It's a good job our calves names are still right."

"Aye and they got wed on the same day as Dick, but I'll tell yee later."

"This is a day I'll never forget, and this cart looks wonderful."

"It sure does, if I say so myself."

He kissed her again before setting off.

"Leave the cart so everyone can see it, the yard's big enough for all the others."

"What about the milking?" Tom gasped.

"Everyone will go before dark, and then you and Dad can do it."

"Aye so let's go in, I want to be alone with yee till they all come."

She giggled as he lifted her down, kissing her passionately before carrying her inside. He knew that it would take some time for everyone to get there.

Bob's cart eventually arrived, followed by William's carriage, so they could get Dick out.

Peg's, came next with Dinah, Harry and Maggie. Two other carts carrying all the others from church soon arrived, and everyone agreed that the cart looked spectacular.

"I'll take all this off the cart and settle Daisy down, she's done well today." Harry said. "When they've got Dick in the house safely, will you see to the others Maggie?"

"They'll need something to eat, and also a drop of your Elderberry wine Harry."

After all the introductions were over, everyone tucked into the delicious spread of sandwiches, pies, tarts and cakes waiting for them .Dick got comfortable in Harry's chair by the fire, and Molly fussed over him. Bob and Dinah went outside for some fresh air and then he heard Harry's tuneless whistling, and froze to the spot.

"What's the matter Bob, you look like you've seen a ghost."

"Stay here Dinah," He muttered. "I'll nere be long."

He dashed into the house, and as Harry passed her coming from the stable he asked. "What are you doing out here?"

"I'm waiting for Bob," She said. "We just wanted some fresh air."

Harry nodded and went inside; it was then that she heard such a commotion going on that she returned to see Bob and Dick shaking Harry's hand as if he was a long lost friend.

"It was Harry's cart that drove me and Dick last year," Bob explained. "We hid in it to cross the river safely and we nay kenned it till now."

"How do you know?"

"Dinna yee hear him whistling in the stable?"

"But lots of people whistle, how did you know it was Harry?"

"People whistle in tune usually, Harry's is out of tune."

Dinah gaped and he continued.

"We asked him if he delivered milk to the Manor house, and he did. What's so strange is that on his way back he met Tom, and then his wheel came off."

"You'd never believe it, would you?" Dinah gasped.

They remained outside cuddling and kissing.

"I've missed you Bob, but after Dick's accident you'll be there for a long time."

"Aye but Molly can nay leave Dick, to teach me to run the mill so she'll need help."

"What are you saying?"

"Emily, Alice and Molly are talking to Peg about it right now. Molly wants you to come and look after Dick, and then we can be together."

"I'd love to, but I can't leave Mum to run the stall alone, can I?"

"She's nay alone, Jim and Nellie will do what yee did, canna they?"

"But Nelly's having a baby and she can't help for long."

"If we'd got wed and it was yee having a bairn," He argued. "It's just the same."

"Your right, they should and I'll go and speak to Mum about it right now."

"Yee can come back with us; I canna stand nay seeing yee everyday."

"Let's go and talk to her, she can't say no, seeing Dick like he is."

They returned to the crowded house, Peg was deep in conversation with the three wives and their husbands were catching up while Maggie chatted to the Bradmans.

Harry was liberally plying the group from church with his Elderberry wine and they were all laughing and enjoying themselves.

"What've yee two been up to?" Dick shouted from Harry's chair, to their discomfort.

"We needed some fresh air and its cooler out there."

Peg's face was flushed and Dinah hoped that the women had not upset her.

"Aye and it'll be getting dark soon, we'd best be away home; it's a shame to break this grand do up. Get Molly, from them gossiping women, so we'll get back to the mill."

"Leave it Dick," Tom said. "Yee ken what's going on?"

"Sorry Tom I forgot, but I'm afeared of that journey back tonight."

"Why not stay here?" Tom said. "Bob will drive whoever goes back with him tonight. Alice and I can take yee back tomorrow; it'll give us some time alone on the way back." "What'll Molly say about it?" Dick asked.

"Leave it to me." Tom said. "I'll go and find out how they've have gone on with Peg."

He arrived just as Dinah was about to confront her mother, but he spoke first.

"Dick needs yee Molly, and I need my wife."

144

Emily's tact and diplomacy had worked, and Dinah turned to Bob in frustration.

"Just a minute young lady," Peg called. "We've to talk, if you'll excuse us, Emily?" "Yes Peg, I will find William he must think I have deserted him."

Leaving Peg, Emily glanced at Ruth and Martha chatting contentedly to Maggie, and went to tell William the outcome.

"You want to stay the night Dick?" Molly gasped. "And not come home with us?"

"Aye if Harry and Maggie agree, I canna face that journey again tonight."

"What, happens if you need anything in the night, Dick?"

"We're in the next room," Tom said. "Harry and I can lift him upstairs, and Maggie will see to all his needs."

He then saw Bob hugging Dinah and swinging her around.

"Aye it looks like she's coming, so yee'll sleep better Molly, nay worrying about him."

"It was all William's idea, Molly said. " Why didn't we think about it before? Thanks to all of you and I'm so glad that Dinah's staying, not just for our sake, but for Bob's. I've not felt well lately, it must be the shock of the accident."

"Look, the party's breaking up," Dick noticed. "Yon lads are off with Queeny and Alf."

William, Emily and the Bradmans were the next and thanked Harry and Maggie for having them and asked them to go over to Freestone and visit them at some point.

"I am so pleased to have met Williams's brothers and both of you too. Like Molly, I too have nobody close by; and it is so nice to belong to a large family." Emily added.

Maggie and Harry acknowledged them. But then William turned to his brothers.

"Yee take care Dick, and yee too Molly. I hope we'll be at yon wedding soon Bob and Dinah, I expect we'll meet at the auction some time Tom, unless yee come to visit us?"

"Aye and thanks for being my best man William, but it'll nay be till the bairns born."

They all waved until they were completely out of sight.

It was Peg's turn next; she too thanked Maggie and Harry, and wished Dinah well.

She also did the same for Bob, Tom, Alice, Dick and Molly, before leaving.

They all waved her off too. Bob, Dinah and Molly remained she didn't like leaving Dick. "Are you sure about this Maggie? It'll be hard, and you've all this to clear up."

"Stop fretting lass, there's four of us here and I'm sure we'll manage, you do?"

"Get going or it'll be dark when yee get back." Dick urged. "I'll see yee tomorrow."

"Aye he's right." Bob said. "Or I'll end up in the river, come on Dinah."

She nodded adding her thanks to everyone and to Alice for allowing her to be a bridesmaid before they eventually left. The night was drawing in as the four of them waved them off, Dick remained seated till they returned.

"Go to bed Alice," Tom said. "We've milking to do and get this man upstairs first."

"Less of that yon cheeky thing," Dick replied. "But thanks for letting me stay, I canna have stood that journey back tonight."

"Put him in your old room Tom," Maggie said." I'll bring up what he needs."

146

"Goodnight all," Alice shouted. "If you need anything Dick, Tom can see to it."

"I dinna expect yee to Alice," Tom laughed. "Nay in your condition, so I'll be up later."

He and Harry lifted Dick carefully up to his room, while Tom put him into bed.

"Sorry to spoil yon honeymoon Tom; yee must think I'm a damn nuisance?"

"It's nay a honeymoon," Tom said. "Not with Alice as she is, but we'll make up for it."

"Thanks Tom, I'd nay have missed seeing yee wed, or meeting William again. We've come along way in less than a year, remember that snow? I thought we'd have all died of cold in a ditch somewhere. Have yee still got yon stone? I have, and it was lucky for me, till this week anyway."

"Aye I've got mine and it brought me luck," Tom admitted. "Yee stone still has Dick."

"How do yee work that out?" Dick asked. "Just look at me."

"Yee might have been killed," Tom said. "Yee'll get over this yee are a strong man."

"Aye we must all be surviving the war, now each of us has found happiness."

"And we met up again today, dinna we? But now get some sleep. Yee need yee strength for tomorrow, goodnight Dick, shout if yee need me."

"Night Tom, and thanks for all yee've done for me, all of my life."

"Yee are welcome," Tom blanched   "It was my place to do it."

Dick's words lingered, and yet he could not tell him why. By the time he went downstairs the table was cleared and Maggie had washed up.

"Do you think Dick will be all right?"

"Think so Maggie, he's tired but he has that bottle for the pain if he needs it."

"You get off to bed, Harry's done the milking? Have you enjoyed your day?"

"Aye it's been grand, but I dinna expect all that happened, and thanks for everything, but I'm sorry I wasna down in time to help."

"Never mind that Tom, you've helped all your brothers today."

"All, of them, how?" He questioned.

"Because you got William here which helped Bob and Dinah to get together, then helping Dick as you've just done which in turn helps Molly."

"I dinna do it on my own." He flushed. "The three women helped."

"You had a hand in it, didn't you?" Maggie insisted.

"Aye, I suppose so," He nodded. "But yee have to help dinna yee?"

You're a nice man Tom, and I'm glad that you're my son in law."

"Thanks Maggie, but it's time we were away to bed, isna it?" He blushed.

"Yes son, goodnight." She added.

Harry entered then after finishing the milking.

"Night Maggie, yee too Harry, and thanks for doing that."

They dragged themselves upstairs after a long and exhausting day, one they would all remember for a long time.

Harry and Maggie were up and had finished their breakfast, when Tom came down. "Did yee take the leaves off the cart last night, Harry?"

"Yes I did it after we came back from church, but I'll get the cart ready Tom, will you get Dick dressed and take his breakfast up? I'll help to get him down after. You and Alice have your breakfast together first."

148

"Thanks Harry, we three brothers owe yee our lives that day."

"You've repaid me many times, even making me into a granddad."

He respected Harry for that, as he went to see to Dick. Alice was asleep so he left her; it was going to be a long day by the time they returned home from Cunningham.

Maggie came in with a plate.

"Here's Bob's breakfast take it, he needs building up."

"Thanks Maggie "I'll wake Alice too so we can have ours, afore Harry gets back."

"Harry and I talked this morning, about how strange life is. Apart from him saving the three of you that day, he helped Molly`s dad in the mill when her mother fell while expecting her, and our Alice, Molly, Emily and me, are all an only child."

"Folks would nay believe it," Tom gasped. "Would they?"

"They certainly wouldn't," Maggie agreed. "But I've been thinking, you'll not get to Cunningham before dinner, so I'll do some bagging for you all."

"Thanks Maggie, did Molly leave any covers for Dick, in the cart?"

"Yes, I've kept them warm by the fire all night, did Dick sleep well?"

"I dinna hear anything so he must have, I went in but he was still asleep. I'll go and dress him when he's eaten, so we'll see yee later."

After he'd sorted Dick out, he woke Alice by kissing her cheek, she opened her eyes. "Morning Mrs Cardell, are yee ready for our first married breakfast together?"

"And which breakfast, shall we have first Mr Cardell?" Smiling, she dragged him onto the bed, and he offered no resistance, it was their honeymoon after all.

"Come on yee hussy, we canna stay here all day, nay that I'd mind."

"What a shame," She sighed. "I'll get dressed as fast as I can, unless you help me?"

"We'll nay get anything done if I do;" Tom smirked. "We've a big day ahead of us."

"Spoilsport," She pouted. "I'll be down in no time, has Mum got our breakfast ready?" He nodded and reluctantly left, she made him happy, he hoped nothing would spoil it.

They enjoyed their breakfasts and Maggie hovered not knowing how to treat them.

"Aye that was grand Maggie; I'll get Dick ready and when Harry comes we'll be away."

"I'll clear the table, and Mum, just be normal with us, all right?"

Maggie smiled, just as Harry returned and went up to help Tom to bring Dick down.

"Thanks Maggie, that's the first time I've felt like eating, it must be yon cooking? But dinna tell Molly I said that."

"It's our little secret Dick," Maggie winked. "But did you sleep well?"

"Aye I did that, but Molly worries in case by moving she hurts me."

"Why not sleep downstairs?" She suggested. "It must hurt going up and down?"

"Aye Maggie it does, but I dinna want to upset, Molly."

"Where's Dinah going to sleep; now she's there?"

"We do have three bedrooms?"

"I'll ask Alice to have a word; you just leave it to us women."

150

"We men are putty in their hands," Dick laughed. "Dinna yee agree, Harry?"

"I let them have their own way, Tom'll soon know that."

Tom flushed remembering what happened this morning, and understood what he meant. "You'd best wrap up Dick it's nippy out, and this time of year it can snow." Maggie said and turned to Alice. "Come and help me to make Dick's bed up so he won't get cold."

After it was ready, he and Harry lifted Dick safely on to the cart.

"I've made some bagging if you're hungry, and there's a warm drink wrapped in your bedding, in case you feel cold, Dick."

"Yee've been so kind Maggie, Tom's lucky having yee to mother him. I canna remember ours having much chance to. Bye and thanks for everything, one day I will repay yee somehow."

"You're welcome Dick, now take care and do have a safe journey home."

They waved until the cart turned onto the lane; Daisy's gentle swaying lulled him to sleep. Alice cuddled up to Tom, travelling in a contented silence so as not to disturb him. He slept while passing the river at high tide, it sent a cold shiver down Tom's back again. "It was like this when all those men drowned last year. Harry heard that all those who did make it across were killed in a place called Culloden, by the English."

"I'm glad you stayed," Alice sighed. "Or we'd not have met and then got married."

He squeezed her tightly, and checked that Dick was still asleep; he only woke as they turned down towards the mill.

"Nay are we here I must've slept. Maggie's jar kept me warm."

The three of them rushed out to meet them.

"You've done well, come in there's a blazing fire and warm soup waiting." Molly said.

Bob helped Alice down, and she went in with Dinah, as Tom and Bob lifted Dick into the house, settling him by the fire. Bob then threw a blanket over Daisy and gave her a drink and some oats, while Molly brought Dicks soup in on a tray.

"How was it last night, I worried about you, but I did sleep well in the end?" Molly said.

"Aye and I did too; maybe I should sleep downstairs until my leg's better? That way we'll both get some sleep while I'm like this dinna yee think?"

"I understand," Molly sighed. "But what if you need anything in the night?"

"Then I'll ring old Sam's bell like he used to."

"I dinna mind helping yee up and down Dick," Bob said. "I ken that it hurts but if yee want I'll bring that single bed down for yee?"

"If you do, then where's Dinah going to sleep?"

"You and Dinah could share," Alice suggested. "That's if it's all right?"

"It's fine with me," Dinah replied. "But how do you feel, Molly?"

She agreed to give it a try, and after they had all eaten Tom offered to help him to bring it down before he and Alice left.

"Thanks Tom," Bob said. "I ken yee've to go soon, but we all enjoyed yon wedding and meeting William, Emily, and the Bradmans, its grand everyone got on so well."

"It worked out for me too, thanks for talking Mum into letting me stay?" Dinah said

"We women can do anything we set our minds to," Alice said. "Can't we Molly?"

"Yes, but the art of it is, to let other people think it's their idea, isn't it?"

152

"Are we getting this bed down Bob?" Tom asked.

Molly and Dinah tided up the space, while Alice washed up.

"Thank yee both," Dick said. "We'll be fine now, till I'm back on my feet."

"Take it easy Dick," Tom said. "Remember there's three watching yee now so we'll see yee all next year, and we'll see what happens to all of us then."

The three of them waved them off and Tom and Alice stopped by the river, to remember the time that they had originally consummated their relationship.

Chapter 13 William

It was a cold November night, when the carriage arrived back at Freestone. The women went straight to bed, while William put the horse and carriage away. They had all agreed that Tom and Alice's wedding was a success, except for poor Dick's accident.

At breakfast the next day with Emily, William explained.

"I think Ruth and Martha should stay in bed, after that long tiring day, dinna yee?"

"Yes you are right; I'll manage the school till Martha does come."

"Are yee asking Mary, if any of yon parents want to learn to read?"

"I will, when she comes, are you going alone to Lymouth today?"

"Aye, now yee've taught me my numbers, so I'll see yee later."

He kissed her and he went to do his chores, Emily let the children into school and waited to ask Mary about her plan.

"Good morning Mary, might I have a word with you before lessons begin?"

"It's funny but I wanted to speak to you too, but you go first Emily."

She outlined her plans.

"So, could ask any ladies from church?"

"Yes, but speaking of church, I've something to tell you."

"What do you mean?"

"It's Reverend Markham; he wants a single lady to do my job and live in the stockroom, to be on call any time. He'll not have my children in the vicarage, so after school they've to help Charles with his duties.

154

I've just to keep the church clean, it's less hours and there's not enough money to pay the rent."

"Oh Mary," Emily gasped. "Whatever will you do?"

"When the new housekeeper comes, I'll not have job. I don't know what'll happen if the Reverend Markham's lah di dah wife ever has a child."

"He will have no choice then, but when is this new housekeeper coming?"

"The beginning of the year, but what can I do about it he's the Squire's son? He never speaks when I'm there and Charlie says he's the same with him, just gives his orders for the day, without a please or thank you."

"Try not to get upset Mary, I am sure it will sort itself out."

"Thanks Emily," Mary sniffed. "You must think I'm being silly?"

"Indeed you are not, you must be worried sick? I will try and help if I can."

"You're so kind Emily, just like your father was. But, I must go or Reverend Markham will wonder where I am."

Emily wished her well and returned to the class, but it was late when Martha did arrive.

"Ruth's got a cough from being out so late so I couldn't leave her."

"Oh dear Martha, is she taking anything for it?"

"Yes, I've given her lots of drinks, but I'm really worried."

"What a day for bad news, and Reverend Markham has upset Mary."

"He was so rude to your father that day, I didn't like him then."

"The problem is that he is the Squires son, so what can I do about it."

"Your right, he shouldn't treat his workers like that? But I must check if Ruth's all right, and I'll try to get back."

"I will make the meal tonight Martha, so do not worry about that."

The class had finished for the day and Mary waited with her children.

"Are you feeling any better, Mary?"

"Not really, as the Reverend was angry that I'd been away so long."

"Oh! Mary, and now Ruth is poorly and Martha left early too."

"I'm sorry about Ruth, Emily, but I'd better go or he'll be angrier."

She wished her well again but Mary didn't answer and after watching them go, she returned to the house just as Martha came downstairs.

"Is Ruth any better?"

"I think that the rest and drinks did the trick, I'm sorry for leaving you."

"You did right to look after her, I am sure she will recover."

Martha wept with worry and Emily held her.

"Come and sit down, you are not alone."

Martha brightened and hoped that Ruth did improve.

Christmas fast approached along with the frost and snow. The school closed because of it, giving Emily and Martha time to prepare the goose and do some baking.

She worried about William driving through the snow; but they were so busy she just carried on. A loud knocking came on the front door, and Emily opened it.

There stood the angry chiselled face of Reverend Markham.

"Mrs Emily Cardell, I would like a word with you."

"Just what is it that you have to say Reverend Markham?"

"I would prefer not to discuss it on the doorstep, if you do not mind."

"I am afraid that we are extremely busy baking for Christmas."

"Even so, if you could spare just a few moments of your time?"

Reluctantly, she agreed showing him into the parlour and asked him what it was about.

"It concerns this so called **school,** which you run."

"Just what has my school got to do with you, may I ask?" She enquired.

"Quite a lot as it happens, have you had permission to open this **school?**"

"Pray tell me Reverend Markham, after running this **school** for two months, who do I require permission from?"

"Why from the Squire my Father of course." He smirked.

"Why, should I require the Squire's permission, it is not on his land?" She retaliated.

"As you so rightly say it is not on his land, but the parents of the children you teach, do live and work on his land."

"What difference, should that make to the Squire?"

"The difference is my Father does not want his workers educated."

"Are you serious? Having workers that can read and write will only benefit him surely."

"These children are the next generation of labourers, and they will not accept the same terms of employment as their ignorant parents have."

"By that," She was stunned. "Do you mean that they will expect better terms?"

157

"When you put it like that, yes, I suppose that is exactly what I mean."

"So what you are saying is that nobody should better themselves, that they should be satisfied with the continuing exploitation of the working class?"

"I would not say that, it is more like being grateful to be employed." He stammered.

"Can I take it Reverend that you are acting for your father on this matter?"

He shuffled awkwardly and she jumped on his discomfort to attack him again.

"So this objection to my **school** is purely personal then, is it?"

"Yes, my workers neglect their duties, bringing their children to your **school.**"

"So what this means, is that you expect your workers, or shall we say your employees, to work day and night for you?"

"These people should be glad to have a job, whatever the terms."

"These people have families to care for and rents to pay, they are not animals, and even they have a break."

"You are a bad example to the working class, Mrs Cardell."

"And you sir, are a bad example to the ministry you studied for."

"You are only a vicar's daughter, how dare you question my faith?"

"Your have no faith sir. If you truly believed the teaching of the church, you could not behave so badly to your employees, or your congregation."

His face flushed at her audacity talking to him like that in his position.

"How dare you madam? I have never been so insulted in my life."

She grinned and persisted.

"Well sir, perhaps it is time that someone reminded you, that God said love me and your neighbour as yourself."

"If I needed any advice regarding my belief madam, you would be the last person I would listen to."

"Perhaps sir, I might be the only person brave enough to tell you."

"Brave madam, or foolish, it remains to be seen."

During this altercation, a thought suddenly struck her.

"Something has just occurred to me sir; you never wanted to be a minister did you? It must be hard being the third son, not having any choice in your own future."

He was dumbfounded at her knowledge of his situation, yet she continued.

"My Father chose to be a minister, because he loved God and his neighbour, which is why everyone loved him."

"Then indeed your father was a lucky man, I had no choice."

"You do have a choice; you can do something else, or stay and make a difference."

His manner then changed making him admit everything.

"How can I leave, my Father would disinherit me?"

"So what you are saying is that your father's money is more important, than yours and everybody else's happiness, is that right?"

He conceded that there was some truth in her assumptions.

"When ... you put it like that, it must be. I have been so miserable and my poor wife blames herself."

"So Reverend, what are you going to do? In two days it will be Christmas, the day of our Saviour's birth, is it going to be a new birth for you?"

"I do not know Mrs Cardell; I need time to consider my options."

"The people here need a minister who cares about them, if it is not going to be you, then perhaps it is time that you left."

He rose ready to go, just as the door suddenly flung open and standing there was William.

"Why are yee, shouting and upsetting my wife?"

"Reverend Markham is leaving William. "We have been speaking frankly and now he must decide what course of action to take."

"I'd have told him what people thought of him, the first day we met."

"I am aware of people's ill feeling towards me, Mr Cardell. Do I care, it remains to be seen."

He grabbed his coat, and she saw him out.

"Let us know, if there is a service on Christmas day?" She asked and on closing the door she collapsed and William rushed and carried her into the parlour and shouted.

"Martha come quickly and stay with Emily, while I get the doctor."

On his arrival he examined her with Martha in attendance; he told Emily what it was.

"I've seen the doctor out now William and have settled up with him." Martha said.

William then hurried into the parlour where Emily explained everything to him.

"Yee are having a .... bairn Emily! I'm glad there's nothing wrong with yee. But when's it due? And are yee all right?"

"I am quite well William, the doctor said that it is quite normal to feel light-headed, because of our tight clothes. He said that it will be born, in the summer."

"I canna believe we're having a bairn. I dinna care, if yon mon stays or not, do yee?"

"It remains to be seen, but it will not spoil our joy."

"I'll bet Martha's already told Ruth the news, dinna yee?"

"Can you blame her as the news might just make her feel better.

It was indeed the case, because on Christmas morning William helped Ruth down.

"I'm so glad to be back and congratulations on your news, isn't it exciting? Martha was the last baby to be born here and that was years ago."

"All right Ruth, don't say anymore and remember your five years older than me."

William and Emily laughed to hear their banter.

"A Happy Christmas to you both, we have really missed you Ruth."

After breakfast they exchanged gifts.

"What time are you all going to church?" Ruth enquired

"I'll stay with you Ruth, I don't know if William and Emily are going."

A knock came at the door again and William opened it then, to a snow covered Mary.

"A Happy Christmas to you all, Reverend Markham wants you to know that the service is at 10.30, and he hopes that you'll both come. You'll never believe it; he's looking after my children till I return."

"A Happy Christmas to yee too Mary and yee do look much happier today."

"I should be, the Reverend wants me to stay and he's letting us ladies do our charitable work in the parish stockroom. I don't know who or what made him change, but whoever it was did us a big favour."

"I'm glad to hear it Mary, and thanks for coming and I'll tell Emily."

He watched Mary skip down the path with a smile so warm, it could melt the snow.

161

He returned to tell everyone the news, and smiled at Emily who then said.

"We had better go before the service starts; Christmas is indeed a time for miracles."

"Yes and three miracles have happened today, Ruth's back with us, you're having a baby, and the Reverend is staying." Martha said.

"Why wouldn't he stay, he's the Squire's third son and it's his duty." Ruth asked.

"I'll tell you about it Ruth, when William and Emily have gone."

On their arrival the service had already started, so they slid into the back bench.

Christmas always brought the whole village together, and the Squire and his family sat in the front pew. At the homily Reverend Markham smiled at them, before addressing the congregation.

"I would like to wish you all a happy and Holy Christmas, and to thank you all for coming to celebrate the birth of our Saviour. I hope it will be the birth of new beginnings for all of us. We welcome God into our life, and must never take our faith for granted. Do continue in the New Year to attend the Sunday services. I assume you all like my own family will celebrate the Lord's birthday with your own families."

The congregation clapped, at the miraculous change in their minister.

After the service Reverend Markham and his wife greeted everyone, saving a special moment for Emily and William.

"May God bless you both, I might also add, Emily that you are indeed a formidable woman."

She blanched, and William answered.

"Thanks Reverend, I agree with yee."

He noticed how tightly Elizabeth Markham grasped Emily's hand as they left.

"It seems William that things are looking very promising for all of us in 1747."

*   *   *

In the New Year William became concerned about Emily's future.

"What will yee do Emily, when yon school opens?"

"That is what worries me?" She bit her lip. "As my clothes do not fit me anymore."

"Why not ask Ruth and Martha if they can make something for yee?"

"A good idea, I will ask them as it is hard to breathe in what I am wearing now."

After their meal William went into the parlour to let Emily talk to Ruth and Martha. "Could you please help me, I need something to wear for when the school opens?"

"Martha and I have waited ever since you fainted before Christmas, but we can't get out in this weather to buy any material."

"What can I do then?"

"We could alter one of your dresses Emily, what do you think?" Martha suggested. "I'll bring one down right away; maybe I can help if you will show me how?"

She eagerly dashed upstairs.

"I hope you know what to do?" Ruth enquired.

"We'll think of a way, nothings beaten us yet has it Ruth?"

Emily returned with the green outfit that she wore for Tom and Alice's wedding.

"Will this do?"

"But Emily, it's your best dress, are you sure?" Ruth questioned and Martha was agog. "It is no good

163

keeping it just for best; I need something to wear right now."

"If you're sure, then we'll start to unpick all the seams." Ruth said.

When they finished they folded up all the pieces neatly, and Emily's heart sank to see it.

Ruth then armed with a long cord suggested.

"I'll measure your waist and then make it much bigger; to last till the baby arrives."

"Bigger! How big will I get?" Emily gasped.

"Women having babies always keep out of sight until they've had it." Martha explained. "So why is that?" Emily asked.

"For the same reason as you, their clothes don't fit them anymore." Martha continued.

"But I cannot keep out of sight if I am to run the school, can I?" Emily retorted.

"I'm afraid that you'll have to give up the school quite soon." Ruth tactfully explained.

"But if I let the school go, I will have no income, will I?" Emily sighed.

"Then someone else must run it, say like Mrs Markham." Ruth suggested.

"I had not thought that far ahead, but I will ask her later."

They soon marked out material to see how much was needed for an extra wide skirt.

"The material that's left we will make a brat with sleeves. It'll mean no more tight waists and full skirts for a while Emily." Ruth explained.

"Whatever is a brat, Ruth?"

"It's a top to wear over your skirt and will hide your tummy."

Emily nodded eager to learn even though neither of the sisters had attempted it before.

"We'll wrap the skirt round your waist leaving enough to let it out." Ruth said.

The three worked hard until the design was completed, and it was fastened by a button.

"You are both so clever, but why has nobody ever thought of this before?"

"Don't they say that necessity is the Mother of invention?" Martha replied.

"Soon the brat, with the sleeves was all sewn up and Emily paraded in front of them.

"It's so comfortable and I want to go and see Elizabeth right now."

Fortunately William had just arrived back from Lymouth and put the empty cart away. "My, dinna yee look smart? When yee ladies start something nothing gets in the way."

"Thank you, kind sir." They all curtsied and then Emily explained her plan to him.

"Elizabeth Markham!" He gasped. "She'll nere come here to run the school."

"Where else can she run it?" Emily asked.

"We'll soon find out, I'll take yee when I get the carriage ready."

"That would be nice, William, thank you." She smiled.

On their arrival Emily asked Elizabeth and she agreed, Reverend Markham did not.

"The school should be in the church stockroom; it is more convenient for my wife."

"If yee think I'm lugging everything back here, yee mun think again." William reacted.

"You can keep them, because the Squire will pay for anything that we need?"

"We should go Emily?" William ranted. "The bairns will be taken care of now."

165

Emily was deflated and rode home in silence, and told Ruth and Martha her worries.

"Didn't Mary, say that the ladies were using the stockroom?" Martha asked.

"What am I to do now?" She wept on Williams's shoulder.

"Use the outhouse, we'll show the ladies how to make clothes like yours." Martha said

Ruth was shocked, William was lost for words, and Emily had a thought.

"I can show mine to the draper in Freestone and he might just let us have some material, if we agree to sell him the finished article, at a price to suit us all."

Martha and Ruth gaped in astonishment

"Do you mean that we should go into business, at our age?" Ruth gasped.

"You only need to see that everything is done properly." Emily explained.

"I'm sure all the ladies could do with some extra money, Ruth." Martha suggested.

"They can still do their charitable work if they want to, I suppose." Emily added.

"So they can, and it'll bring some money in, after losing the school." Ruth agreed.

"Aye and when the bairn comes, there'll be enough of yee to care for it." William said.

Next day after the milking and the ladies finished their chores and before going to Lymouth, they all could go into the drapers shop together. He went to ensure that the arrangements were mutually satisfactory, for their business to succeed. He then recalled Emily's words on Christmas day that 1747 was going to be a promising year for all of them.

Chapter 14 Dick

The liming of the mill had to remain unfinished; because Molly began to teach Bob how to run it.

"The only difference between you and Dick is that you know about money." She said.

"Aye I was lucky meeting Peg, but it's grand having Dinah as a nurse and housekeeper to relieve yee, isna it?"

"You're right about that Bob, so when the doctor comes to see Dick, she's with him."

In the house after the doctor had examined him, Dick explained his anxieties.

"Molly's nay slept properly since the accident; will yee look at her?"

The doctor agreed and then asked Dinah.

"Will you get Molly from the mill and stay while I examine her?"

She nodded and soon returned with an anxious looking Molly.

"What's the matter doctor is something wrong with Dick?"

"No, actually he is progressing well, but it will be months before he can work in the mill again. It is you that I am concerned about Molly, the shock's taken its toll on you, so I would like to examine you before I leave?"

"There's nothing wrong with me doctor that a few good nights sleep won't cure."

"I think Molly that you and I both know there is more than that bothering you. If you will go upstairs with Dinah, I will be up in just a moment."

"But, we can't leave Dick alone, what if he needs anything?" She fretted.

"Nay lassie I'll manage, now let the doctor have a look at yee, if only for my sake."

Seeing how worried he was Molly agreed, so she and Dinah went upstairs. Dick remained alone feeling anxious until the doctor came back down.

"Aye and is she all right doctor?"

"Molly will tell you," He smiled. "So I bid you good day Dick and I will see you soon."

"Bye doctor and thanks." He responded and then waited patiently until they came down and then Dinah left them to go and see Bob.

"Tell me what he said?" Dick blurted out.

"He said that when you're back on your feet, you'll become a father."

"What!" He gasped. "Me, a father to a bairn! But yee dinna look very happy about it?" "Of course I am," She then explained. "But, what if I end up like Mother?"

"Like yee mother?" He questioned. "And in what way is that?"

"She fell down the mill steps and hurt her back and she then almost lost me. After I was born the doctor said she couldn't have any more babies and I'm afraid the same will happen to me? I hated being an only child and it worries me."

"Molly my love, I'll nay let anything like that happen to yee, besides Bob and Dinah are here now. And when Bob kens how to run the mill, Dinah will help yee in the house. When I'm back on my feet, me and Bob will finish off the mill and the run it together.

If they get wed and have bairn's yee women can bring them up, what do yee say?"

"I do love you Dick," She smiled. "You've thought of everything, but we've to ask them first if they'll stay."

As if on cue, Bob and Dinah came in and congratulated them on their news.

"Aye and at last there's some grand news, we're pleased for yee both. And if yee want us to go by then, we will find somewhere else to live."

"Go, what for?" Dick gasped. "We're a team all four of us, yee can stay here for ever. Yee can get wed when yee like as this is your home too. But we've nay finished the mill yet, and yee did promise to help me dinna yee?"

"Nay dinna feel yee must say that, but I'd like nothing better."

Dinah wept for joy and Bob continued.

"Aye we'd love to stay, but we'll nay get wed until yee can be my best man, Dick."

"And I want you as my matron of honour Molly." Dinah added. "Then we'll be real sisters, even if you've to push the baby down the aisle."

The four of them laughed and eventually shared the best Christmas the mill had seen for a long time. Peg was invited too, but the heavy snowfall made her decision easy. There were less and less farmers braving the winter elements to empty their barns. Only the occasional villager called in for a sack of flour to do their Christmas baking.

*   *   *

By early March Dick was walking with the aid of a stick.

"If yee and Dinah want to get wed, do it afore the mill gets busy. We'll get down the aisle somehow, if Molly dinna explode afore then. Go to yon minister tomorrow."

"Aye yee're right we've waited too long, but I'll want Tom and William to be there."

169

"Aye and if yee get wed at the end of March; it's only three weeks away. Take yon cart and find William at Freestone and ask them all to come."

Bob rushed out to tell Dinah as she hung out the washing, and when Molly returned from the kitchen she saw Dick smirking.

"And just what have you been up to, you're looking very pleased with yourself?"

"Bob and Dinah are to be wed and I said they should do it afore the mill gets busy. Or it'll mean them having a winter wedding just like us."

"I can't be her matron of honour, not the size I am." She was appalled.

"Yee're having a bairn Molly," He laughed. "Yee should put weight on lassie, but if yee're worried, we'll ask yon doctor tomorrow."

"And so I will if you'll only stop going on about it! But we've to put on a spread for them if they do get wed; only I'm not up to baking right now."

"Nay worry, Dinah will help but there will nay be many coming. If Tom and the family canna come it'll only be Peg. Bob's taking Dinah to Freestone in the morning after they've seen yon minister, if they canna, there'll only be a few of us. We'll only need a cake and a few of yon tasty pies."

"Let's just wait and see what happens. But then the sleeping arrangements will better when that bed you're on goes back, and that little bedroom will do nicely for the baby."

In the morning Bob and Dinah returned after seeing the minister and he told them. "It's on the last Sunday in March a week after Easter."

Dick was delighted and Molly concealed her worries.

"Will you be all right while we go to Freestone?" Dinah asked.

170

"Stop fretting, there'll be no farmers around and besides the doctor is coming today." "Make sure you take it easy." Dinah laughed mischievously, and waved.

Later after the doctor had checked Dick, he asked him again.

"Canna yee look at Molly again, she's put so much weight on and I'm afeard about her."

"I will," He agreed. "But where's Dinah?"

"She's away with Bob, canna yee use my bed, if that is all right?"

It was agreed and Molly lay down as the doctor prodded and poked around listening to her tummy though a funnel shaped trumpet and his eyes almost popped out of his head.

"What's wrong doctor is there something wrong with the baby?" She asked in terror.

"No Molly, there is nothing wrong, with either of them in fact."

"Are you saying," She gasped aloud. "That there's … two babies?"

"Yes," He nodded. "And that is why you have put so much weight on Molly, so make sure that you rest and do stop fretting. I shall see you when I visit Dick again. But, no more climbing those mill steps. Not until those babies arrive, and even then it'll be some time before you can go up again, but I will be with you all the way now. "

"Fret, you say?" Molly argued. "Bob can't run the mill yet so we might as well shut it."

The doctor looked concerned.

"If I take my time up the mill steps," Dick suggested. "I'll watch Bob, and Dinah can help Molly in the house."

The doctor mused for a while and eventually said.

"It is not the best idea Dick, not till your leg is healed. But if Bob will see you up and down the steps,

171

anything that eases Molly's mind is worth a try. Only now I've other patients to visit, you talk it over with Bob and Dinah."

When he left, Dick comforted her.

"Come on now Molly lassie dinna fret, I'll look after yee till Bob and Dinah come back, and then we'll all sort it out."

"I'm scared Dick," Molly said. "One baby was enough but two, how will I cope?"

"Yee dinna have to, four of us live here now. Dinah will help yee and I'll help Bob that's what families do. On Skye we brought each another up, Mother would nay have coped with all seven of us surviving bairns."

"I'm glad to belong to big a family," She sighed. "It was lonely being an only child."

"Yee will nay be alone again; this house will be filled with bairns' laughter and tears."

"I love you Dick," She brightened. "And I'm glad you came here that day."

"Aye and so am I, even if yee did give me a hard time, but when yee took off that cap and yee hair fell over yon shoulders, I loved yee then."

"I'm glad we're alone to enjoy our news together." She preened.

"Aye and I hope yon two find Freestone, but it'll be sad if Tom and Alice canna come."

"They should ask them just to see how Alice feels, and then tell them our news."

"Aye we'll speak to them when they come back. But dinna we have talk about names now we've two bairns to think about, is there any yee'd like Molly?"

"I'd like Sam after Dad and Annie after Mother, what would you like?"

"Aye well Sam for one and Thomas after my Father for the other if yon are laddies?"

But if they're lassies Annie's the name of John's twin that died, and Mother was Jennet our sister was named after her but we called her Jinni."

"That's settled then if they're boys Sam and Tom and if they're girls Annie and Jinni."

"Aye but what if it's one of each?" Dick asked.

"Trust you, and I thought we'd done so well till then?"

"Sam for a boy, Annie for a girl," He conceded. "It is their grandparent's mill after all."

Molly's face brightened and she jumped up refreshed to make their evening meal. It wasn't long before Bob and Dinah returned, beaming all over their faces.

"We've so much to tell you have you been all right, and what did the doctor say?" Dinah asked.

"We've something to tell you," Dick ignored them. "So we'll say our news first."

Bob and Dinah were amazed that they didn't want to hear all about William.

"The doctor's been and checked me and Molly."

"Is everything all right?" Dinah asked concerned.

Molly explained with a sparkle in her eye.

"More than all right, we're having twins, what do you think about that?"

Bob seemed uncertain at first.

"Twins just like Mother and Father, does that mean we might have them too?"

Dinah ignored his worries, and was thrilled but then asked.

"Two babies how grand, but will you still want us to stay? Don't you want to have them to yourselves?"

"The doctor won't let me climb the mill steps till after the babies are born. So can you help Dick up and down them Bob, so he can help you to run it? And

Dinah, will you help me with the babies so we can run the house together?"

"It's fine by me," Dinah beamed. "But what do you think Bob?"

"Aye and then we'll work together again Dick. I always thought how nice it would be to live here the first day we came."

"So then we're all agreed that we men will be the Millers and yon women will run the home and have the bairns?"

"I think Bob and I should get married first," Dinah laughed. "Don't you Molly?

They all laughed and then Molly suggested.

"I'll put the kettle on for a drink."

Dinah joined her while Dick chatted to Bob.

"Aye well tell me all yon news? Did yee find Freestone? Are they all coming?" He hardly took a breath with all his questions, which made Bob hope that Dick's memory was now returning, when Molly shouted from the kitchen.

"Hey, don't start telling him yet, I want to hear it too."

The men laughed again and waited for the nettle tea to brew, and then Dick and Molly listened with baited breath to hear all their news.

"We found William in Freestone," Bob began. "And they made us so welcome."

"Emily is having a baby about the same time as you." Dinah interrupted.

"How lovely, only what will she do about the school?"

She and Bob were sworn to secrecy, so she changed the subject.

"Emily's lent me her wedding dress, but I hope you're not upset Molly?"

"I'm not upset; everyone's seen mine that's why I didn't offer it."

Bob was afraid that Dinah might give the show away so he changed the subject.

"So Molly, now there's three of yee having bairns at our wedding."

"But, I can't wear my Father's old clothes to follow Dinah down the aisle." Molly said.

"Dinna worry about that, Molly. When we get my bed back upstairs it'll make some room for yon wedding."

"We only talked about that today, isn't it strange?" Bob said.

"Do it tomorrow Bob, I'm ready for bed now."

"Aye and it's been a long day for us too, shall I take Emily's wedding dress up Dinah?"

"Where have you put it?" Molly questioned

"Behind the door as I didn't want to upset you." Dinah said.

"Put it in your room, till you move into it tomorrow."

"I'm so happy." Dinah sighed.

"You're not as happy as me, to have you here as my sister." Molly smiled.

Bob was thrilled that they got on just like him and Dick, and then took his leave.

"I'll see yee all in the morning."

"Goodnight Bob and Molly remember that I'm back with yee tomorrow night."

"And not before time, it's been nice sharing with Dinah, she'll be glad to sleep alone."

"I'm pleased that you want me to stay, and tomorrow night you'll be together again."

Next morning Bob and Dinah struggled to get the bed up the stairs, before leaving for Bondswick and

175

then onto Blackmoor Moss. Molly changed all the sheets while they were away.

"You're nay washing them lassie, Dinah will go mad with yee?" Dick warned.

"She's enough to do cleaning up, after you've slept down here."

"There's plenty of time afore the wedding, what's all the rush?"

"What's all the rush?" She shouted. "Dinah's to make something for me to wear yet." "Aye and just what do you think Emily and Alice will be wearing?"

"I don't know." She shrugged. "But we'll look bonny sights waddling down the aisle."

"I'll be as bad hobbling down next to Bob." Dick sniggered. "Dinna yee think?"

They cried with laughter until Molly had a thought.

"If Alice does come, the journey could start the baby off."

"They might nay come; we'll wait and see when yon two come back."

"I'll ask the doctor and his wife to come, next time he's here just in case we need him."

"That's bad," Dick frowned. "To ask them just in case anyone might want him."

"I might need him, who knows, besides he's been very good to us."

"Be careful, we dinna want Dinah to worry."

"I'll be careful; I wouldn't upset her for the world."

"It's a pity Peg dinna ask Betty to make yee something."

"There's no time, with the wedding happening so fast."

."Stop fretting Molly lassie, the doctor said you've to rest"

"He's a man, so it's easy for him to say, when there's so much to do."

"Molly, just think about the bairns or yee'll upset them."

"All right, but if Tom and family do come, I don't know what I'll do."

"Don't yee mean what we four will do?"

"I'm tired of worrying, I could do with shutting my eyes."

"Let's have an hour in bed?" He said smiling. "Yee'll feel better after it."

Molly nodded knowing there would be no lovemaking not in their present conditions. They climbed the stairs him with his stick and she with her large tummy. It was months since Dick had seen her undressed and he was shocked.

"I dinna expect four of us to sleep together, is there nay room for me?"

"You cheeky thing, it's all your fault there's four of us anyway."

They eventually stopped laughing; and it wasn't long before they fell asleep. Only to be awakened by the noise Bob had made putting the cart away.

"They're back! We'd better get down as fast as we can." Molly screamed.

"Fast I canna do," Dick laughed. "It'll take time for me to get down yon stairs."

They appeared quite calm, when Bob and Dinah rushed in to share their news.

"We've seen Peg," Bob began. And she's giving Dinah away..."

"She's bringing what she did for your wedding in the food line." Dinah butted in. "and I've brought some pretty pink braid from Betty off the market, if we undo the seams of your fathers white baggy pants and make them into a skirt I'll trim them with it We can also shorten the sleeves of a shirt and shape the neck then trim those, will it do Molly?"

"How clever of you Dinah," She beamed. "Wherever did you get that idea from?" Dinah smiled wryly and didn't say that the Bradmans had suggested it.

"Maggie is making our wedding cake and doing some baking." Bob said.

"So does that mean everyone is coming?" Molly asked.

"It looks like things will work out good for us after all." Dinah said excitedly. "And Alice has had her way about coming"

Molly smiled but didn't mention about asking the doctor and his wife to come to the wedding.

Chapter 15 Bob

The previous day Bob and Dinah had set out on a crisp March morning for Freestone. They headed towards the river where they had met William last November for Tom and Alice's wedding.

"I can't believe we're getting married so soon, I'll have to wear my bridesmaids dress yet again."

"Should we have waited, to give yee time to get a dress?"

"I'd rather not, it doesn't matter what I wear does it?"

Bob nodded and then gulped when passing the Manor.

"Fancy Harry, saving mine and Dick's life that day, but crossing this bridge again still upsets me."

"How far do yee think William travelled?"

"Tom met him at the auction, so we'll ask someone there where Freestone is."

They turned the other way at Queeny Carter's cottage and soon reached the auction.

"Ask those two farmers Bob."

He enquired and they pointed the way to Freestone and when they arrived they asked two ladies where the Bradmans lived.

"There that looks like the cobbled wall, so this must be the cottage." Dinah exclaimed.

Bob knocked on the door and a surprised Martha opened it.

"What a shock seeing you two here, come in we're just getting dinner ready for William's return, he'll be so pleased to see you."

Bob beckoned Dinah who then took in their bagging.

"I insist that you eat with us," Martha was adamant. "There's plenty of mutton stew to go round." They followed her into the kitchen where Ruth and Emily also welcomed them with open arms, as did William when he arrived. Ruth ladled out the portions which they readily devoured.

"Well, this is a nice surprise." William said. "And how's Dick and Molly?"

"He's walking with a stick now," Bob explained. "And Molly's having a bairn in the summer."

"What a coincidence," Emily gasped. "So am I at around the same time."

"Congratulations to you both but Molly's much bigger than you are Emily, is that why you're wearing those strange clothes?"

Emily nodded; she stood up and turned round to show them.

"Ruth and Martha made it and I helped, it is made from the outfit that I wore for Tom and Alice's wedding, do you like it?"

"I've never seen anything like it," Dinah gasped. "I bet its comfortable Emily? Molly's wearing her father's old whites it's all that fits her now and she's worried about what to wear for the...."

"That's why we've come," Bob interjected. "To invite you all to our wedding, in three weeks time."

There was an awkward silence, but he continued.

"Dinah wants Molly as her matron of honour, before she bursts."

They all laughed with relief.

"Have you got a wedding dress yet Dinah?" Emily asked.

"No, so I'll have to wear my bridesmaids dress, it'll have to do."

Emily glanced at the sisters and they nodded their agreement.

"You are welcome to use my wedding dress, it should have been Agnes's but she never wore it, nobody has seen it except us."

"I'd love to Emily, if you think it will fit me?" Dinah`s eyes welled up.

The men walked outside for a chat to let the women see to such things.

William explained what happened when Emily could not cope in her condition with the school. Ruth and Martha had already made her an outfit because her clothes no longer fitted her.

"Aye so what has happened to the school?"

"The vicar's wife now runs it in the Kirk stockroom, so then Emily had no income."

"That is nay good, what did she do then?"

"The ladies of the parish used to make clothes for the poor in there, so they had nowhere to go. Emily suggested they put their efforts into making clothes like hers for ladies having bairns."

"How can that give her an income?"

William then explained how the arrangement with the draper in Freestone worked.

"Molly could do with one for the wedding, but there's nay enough time now."

They strolled idly down the lane chatting together till they reached the shoreline.

"I dinna ken the sea was so near."

That's the way to Lymouth," William pointed. "I take the cart there to sell our produce."

"It's grand to ken where yee ended up, but do yee nay think about what we saw?"

"Aye and I still have nightmares; and I told Emily afore we got wed."

"Dick used to talk about it, but nay since his accident."

"Did yon fall affect his memory?"

"He remembers seeing yee and then spending the night at Blackmoor Moss."

"Aye that's sad, but did Tom ever say anything to yee about it?"

"Nay, but something has upset him I can tell."

"They say that those who swam the river that day last year were all killed at a place called Culloden, or so the Reverend Markham was told by the Squire, his father. What a waste of life for even those who chose to fight, we're the lucky ones to only have scars and nightmares; at least we're still alive."

They were lost in their own thoughts, until Bob suddenly remembered.

"Aye, we'd best be away home or it'll be late when we get back, and we've left Dick and Molly too long, but it's been grand to talk."

He nodded and by the time they arrived back at the cottage, the women were deep in conversation.

"Is everything sorted, Dinah?" Bob asked.

"The wedding dress fits me Bob," She beamed. "But you've to wait till the day. What about Emily and Molly having babies arriving so close together?"

"Aye and it's grand about yeer news," He nodded. "And we've enjoyed being here; Dick and Molly will want to hear everything when we return."

"Thanks for lending me the dress Emily and thank you Ruth and Martha for the advice, we'll see you all in three weeks."

"Don't forget our secret Dinah." Emily reminded her putting her finger to her lips.

She nodded and then waved still holding tight to the parcel as they set off.

"Emily doesn't want Molly to know anything about their new business, because she's making an outfit for her."

Bob nodded absentmindedly as he plucked up the courage to tell her his worries.

"Dinah, there's something yee should know about me. I still have nightmares just like Dick did after his fall and William does too and he told Emily afore they got wed."

"I'll wipe your brow Bob," She kissed him. "I remember seeing how upset Dick was that day."

"Aye and I feel better now; but we'd best get Dick`s bed back upstairs to make room."

"You're right about that, but do you think Dick will let us use the cart again tomorrow, I've to tell Mum and ask her to give me away?"

"Aye and we'll call at Blackmoor Moss after, to see if they'll come too."

As they arrived at the mill they were both in for a shock to hear that Molly was having twins, and though Dinah was thrilled for them, she secretly wished that she'd known that before talking to Emily and the Bradmans. They eventually managed to tell Dick and Molly as much news as they dared. She had also promised Molly that she'd make her look nice for the wedding, with the knowledge that she had gleaned from the Bradmans.

Early next morning they set out for Bondswick, after first struggling to get the bed back upstairs. "I hope Peg's there, I dinna fancy going to the farm and seeing Jim again."

"It's Nellie I feel sorry for, but Mum's usually there, unless she's run out of stock."

He drove on still feeling apprehensive.

"Here's the crossroads where Dick and I parted so it'll nay be long now."

Dinah nodded, and when they reach the market much to his relief Peg was on the stall.

"What are you two doing here?" She enquired haughtily.

"We're getting wed in three weeks Mum." She beamed.

"What's the rush, you're not...." Peg answered.

"My names not Jim; I just want Molly as my maid of honour, before she has the babies."

"Molly's having twins?" Peg gasped aloud. "Whatever is next?"

"Aye, and I want Dick as my best man now he's walking with a stick; it was him who said we should wed afore the mill gets busy."

"Will you give me away Mum?" Dinah asked.

"I can't, Nellie's baby is almost due." Peg replied curtly.

"What happens if Nellie has the bairn, while yee're here?" Bob asked.

"Don't say that." Peg gasped. "But I suppose her parents would have to see to her then."

"If her parents can see to her then," Bob persisted. "Yee can come to the wedding."

"I wouldn't trust them Parkinson's with a cat," Peg responded. "Never mind my grandchild."

"But there'll be nobody there from my family." Dinah begged

"Dinah's father would have done it," Bob reminded her. "So why canna yee?"

The customers had gathered and stared while the stallholders listened intently to the commotion. "All right," Peg relented. "I'll give you away, but I'm coming home straight after. You can tell Molly that I'll bring the same food, I did for her wedding."

"Thanks, for that Mum" Dinah sighed. "We'll see you then, if not before."

Bob took her away to leave a shame faced Peg to her waiting customers.

"I can't believe my Mother at times, but I must see Betty before we go."

She returned clutching her goods and ranted about her mother all the way to Blackmoor Moss.

"We'll have a much better welcome there." She said.

"At least Peg's giving yee away?"

"At the very least, like you say." She huffed.

They drove down the cinder path and Tom opened the door of the farmhouse.

"Aye and to what do we owe this honour?"

They got down, Bob hugged him and Dinah kissed him.

"Wow, yee two should come more often." He joked as they went inside, where Maggie, Harry and an enormous Alice also greeted them.

"Do have some homemade meat and potato pie there's plenty." Maggie fussed.

"We've got some bagging in the cart Maggie." Dinah explained.

"Then have it for your tea when you get back home." She insisted.

They gladly accepted her hospitality after what they'd gone through with Peg. The conversation flowed easily as Alice placed her vast bulk in Harry's armchair.

"We've something to tell yee." Bob began.

"Molly`s having twins." Dinah butted in. "She and Dick are over the moon."

"Twins!" Alice gasped. "When are they due?"

"In the summer and she is so much bigger than you are Alice."

"Aye and dinna yee mean that they're both blossoming Dinah?" Tom reacted.

"I didn't mean to upset you Alice?" Dinah flushed.

"I know I look like a house side," Alice said. "But Molly's got a long time to go yet."

"Aye and we've come to tell yee all that Dinah and I are getting wed in three weeks."

There was another long silence.

"That's good news, but it's a bit quick. isn't it?" Maggie asked.

Bob then explained the reason for it and the atmosphere quickly changed.

"So will yee all come on the last Sunday in March, that's if yee're up to it Alice?"

Maggie and Harry held back and let Tom explain.

"Aye but it's too close to her time."

"Don't I have a say in this?" Alice objected.

"We don't want anything to happen to you on the way." Dinah explained.

"We took Dick back in his condition and drove slowly," Alice argued. "So why not do it for me?" "Dick, wasn't almost having a baby, was he?" Maggie tactfully explained.

Bob and Dinah blushed with embarrassment as Alice persisted.

"You'll all be with me, so why can't I go?"

"I can see our Alice's point about taking our time," Harry said. "She should be all right."

"Suppose the bairn comes on the way?" Tom argued.

"Women have babies every day, some in the fields while they're working, it's quite normal."

Tom knew otherwise but daren't say.

"Molly was worried too!" Dinah said. "It's only because you are so near your time."

"I'm going to your wedding, and that's that!" Alice insisted.

Maggie though unconvinced had to accept defeat.

186

"In that case I'd better start on your wedding cake, tell Molly we'll provide whatever is needed."

Dinah hugged her tightly.

"Maggie thank you, Molly will be glad as she's not up to much right now."

"Tell Dick I'll make some Elderberry wine?" Harry smirked. "He'll be up in no time."

They all laughed with relief that everything was now settled, when Dinah remembered.

"We saw William yesterday and Emily's baby is due at the same time as Molly`s."

Bob then suggested that he and Tom go out for a walk to leave all this chatter behind them.

"William had talked about the nightmares we all still suffer from, do yee have any?"

"Aye every time I think about yon injuries that nearly killed yee all. I dinna leave the farm till Harry hurt his back, that's why Alice and I went to the mill, or I'd nay have met Dick."

He didn't mention the guilt he had carried all those years, but it was too late now to say anything. "After Dick`s fall the doctor found broken bones in his knee, he said they'd been there ages. Dick was rambling thinking that he was still at war. I made up a story about it happening when we were young at the croft." Bob explained.

"It's my fault; when I took out that musket shot on the battlefield."

"Nay Tom, yee saved his life, what's a limp compared to that?"

"Aye I suppose so Bob, but I feel bad that he's suffered it for so long."

At that moment Dinah appeared to say that they should go or they'd be late getting back."

Tom hugged him, before everyone came out to wave them off.

187

Dinah`s mood appeared bright as they set off and he felt better having spoken to Tom. The journey back dragged, and soon the worry lines appeared on Dinah`s face.

"Are yee all right lassie?"

"I'm pleased that everyone is coming to our wedding" She sighed. But..."

"But, what?"

"There'll be three of them having babies."

"Aye we knew that, so what about it?"

"What if Alice has the baby on the way, what if Molly can't get up the isle, what if Emily's outfit doesn't fit her?"

"Dinah my love there's too many ifs, whatever happens we'll get wed? Yee could say what if it rains, or what if yon dress gets spoilt?"

"Are you trying to make me feel even worse?" She gasped.

He stopped the cart and planted a long lingering kiss on her lips.

"Don't let's start something we might just regret Bob?"

"Who's going to regret it?"

"Bob Cardell you're taking advantage of my distress."

"Aye I would if I could; but we're nere alone enough for that."

"Can't we wait a few more weeks; so I can wear my white dress?" She flushed.

"I just wanted to bring a smile back on yon face." He moaned.

"And I suppose it'd bring a smile to your face too, Bob?"

"Aye, and why canna it?"

She preened at his desire for her, and admitted that it was the same for her.

"Just yee wait till our wedding night, there'll be nay stopping me then."

Dinah gulped as she had quite forgotten why they were getting married in the first place.

"Tom said he'd to leave so Alice could get ready for the Kirk, will I have to?"

"No, I'll get ready in Molly's room and won't come down till you and Dick have gone." "Aye well that's all right then."

"You'll have to welcome everyone to the mill? William's carriage will come so Emily can give Molly her outfit, Mum's bringing the food she promised and it'll be the same for Harry and Maggie won't it?"

"Nay lassie, I'd nay even thought about that."

He started the cart again and they finished their journey much happier.

At the mill Bob put the horse and cart away, Dinah waited before they went in to tell them their news, and she suddenly stopped.

"Oh Bob, I've got a strange feeling that everything has been going too well? Suppose something happens to spoil it all?"

"Dinah lassie it'll nay matter what happens so long as we get wed in the end."

"I suppose you're right Bob, besides we've enough to do in the next couple of weeks. A wedding takes lots of preparation usually and we've to get the house ready and I've still to make something for Molly to wear and she doesn't know about Emily's surprise yet." But she still had this terrible foreboding, which she kept to herself. She held his hand and put on a happy face, ready to face Molly and Dick to tell them all their news again.

Chapter 16 March 1747

It was early on the last Sunday of March, at Blackmoor Moss when Tom and Harry finished the milking. That week he had guided the plough over the fields while Daisy pulled it. Harry followed him scattering the seeds and covering them with his foot, to prevent any scavenging birds from stealing them. While inside the farmhouse Maggie gathered all the baking up including her now famous wedding cake. Alice wore the dress her mother wore for their wedding last November. Maggie previously let out the seams to allow for her eight month swollen belly. The men dashed in, washed and changed into their matching shirts.

"I feel bad in this dress," Maggie fretted. "I wore it for Dick and Molly's wedding." "Bob and Dinah won't care whatever you are wearing, so long as you're there."

"Thanks Harry, that make me feel better."

"Are yee sure it's safe for Alice to go so far like she is?" Tom asked.

"Do stop fretting Tom?" Alice answered. "We're going early so we can take our time."

"She's still a month to go yet remember." Maggie said.

"Come on Tom lad; let's get this food on the cart, so we can be off."

They placed everything at the side of the cart and left room for him and Alice to sit on the bedding, which made it comfortable for her to travel on.

Maggie mentioned while sitting up next to Harry.

"Did you put the covers in; we could still have spring showers yet?"

"Yes, Maggie, now do stop fretting, so we can go."

Tom sat with Alice in the back as Daisy steadily turned towards Cunningham.

On the way Alice got angry with him.

"Do stop staring at me Tom, it makes me feel worse."

"I'm sorry lassie, but I'm worried about yon bairn coming early."

"It might have done even at home, so what's the difference?"

"Aye but yee'd nay be in the back of this cart, would yee?"

"Oh Tom, let's just enjoy the wedding and whatever happens, we'll manage."

But his anxieties were etched in his brain about what his father said all those years ago. If Maggie knew the truth, she might not have let them get wed. When he first met Harry, he had then honestly told him the truth about himself.

"You don't have to stop talking Tom," Alice poked him. "I know you're worried about me, but I don't like it when we fall out."

She cuddled up next to him and rested her head on his shoulder.

"Nay I'll nere fall out with yee Alice, yee mean everything to me lassie."

As they past by the river it was at high spring tide, but not as fierce as the winter one he had experienced but it still turned his stomach again. Tom looked for William's carriage, but there was no sign of it.

*　　　　　*　　　　　*

At Freestone on that March Sunday morning things were in full swing ready for the trip to Cunningham. Emily was satisfied that her green skirt and tunic top, looked nothing like the one she wore for Tom and

Alice's wedding. She had earlier wrapped Molly's brown outfit up that they had hurriedly completed, ready to give it to her.

"I've finished my chores," William said as he dashed in to get ready. "And my yee ladies look smart."

"Hurry up William; we must get there in time for Molly to change before the wedding."

"Ruth and I hope Bob and Dinah didn't tell her about our surprise."

"They promised, and anyway Dinah's made something to pacify Molly."

"It's a strange wedding isn't it Emily?"

"Why should you think that, Martha?"

"There'll be four unborn babies at the church."

"We will look like three galleons sailing down the aisle." Emily joked.

"Molly's having twins and Alice is nearly eight months, isn't she?" Ruth said.

"I do hope that Alice will be all right, travelling so near her time."

"She'll be fine as long as she doesn't have the baby on the way." Martha said.

"I think she's very brave going to this wedding" Ruth said. "Now let me take that parcel off you Emily, so it can go in the back of the carriage with us."

"Thank you Ruth," She passed it over. "It might get creased up at the front?"

William then arrived in his Sunday best.

"I'm ready Emily, shall we go now?"

On a beautiful spring morning they set off for Cunningham, to Bob's wedding.

"I bet it's a madhouse at yon mill, I hope Dick gets down the aisle all right."

"Never mind about that William, I wonder what Dinah has made for Molly to wear?"

"It dinna matter; she'll be glad when yee give her what yee've made."

"I hope that she is not offended by it, I would hate to upset her."

"Nay Dinah would have said if she thought that, so dinna worry lassie."

"The draper in Freestone says that we cannot make them fast enough, so all the ladies having babies must like them."

"Aye it was a grand idea going into business; even the sisters seem to be happy now."

"I was worried about them at first, because they said they were too old, but that has not been the case. In fact they now enjoy sharing their skills with the ladies in the outhouse."

"Aye they dinna seem to miss not doing their charity work; and enjoy their new skills."

William turned to see Ruth and Martha chatting in the back of the carriage, this adventure has given them a new lease of life, he thought.

"This weather canna upset Ruth's chest this time, like it did after Tom's wedding."

"Oh! William, I never thought about making something for Alice to wear."

"Nay dinna fret lassie, she'll wear something of Maggie's."

"You are right; she does have a mother to help her, not like Molly and me."

"Aye and talking of mothers, I'll bet Peg's there early to help Dinah out."

"They are both very lucky, but I feel that Ruth and Martha are like mothers to me."

"I've always felt that way, even though they nere had any bairns."

They continued on amiably in the glorious spring sunshine.

"I wonder if we will meet Harry's cart on the way, I bet Maggie's done her famous baking and that lovely wedding cake again?"

"I canna see them," He strained his neck to look. "Aye but passing yon river again hurts and I wonder if the others feel the same way? I still see all those who died and the ones I'd killed, we were all lucky to have survived."

"They too must still have nightmares about it, just like you do."

"Yee'd think I'd have put it all behind me by now, but I'm nay as bad am I?"

"No, you do seem better lately; it only happens if I turn over and touch you sometimes."

"Aye and I was worried about it afore we got wed, in the outhouse nobody heard my screams. It'll have scared Ruth and Martha to death when we moved into the cottage."

"Let us forget it all today, we should feel happy for Bob and Dinah?"

"Aye and we're nearly there, so Molly's got time to change now."

"Look, there is the mill, I wonder if we are the first to arrive?"

"Nay I think Peg will be there as she lives nearer, I bet yons fretting leaving Jim with Nelly as her bairns due the same time as Alice's."

*   *   *

At the mill it was indeed hectic and Dinah was excited about her big day. Molly wore the outfit that she had made out of old Sam's whites. The women were in Dick and Molly's bedroom, while the men were in the room she and Bob would have after they were married.

194

Dinah didn't want to tempt fate, by seeing him before the wedding, but Molly was continuing to stress

"Does this look all right Dinah, I feel and look so fat in it?"

"Just as long as you feel comfortable Molly, that's what really matters."

"But it looks like, goodness knows what."

"How do you think Alice will look?" She sighed. "She's only got a month to go. Emily will be getting big by now too, so you're not the only one that feels fat."

"You're right; but I'll still look a bonnie sight trundling into church behind you, looking such a beautifully slim bride."

Dinah's smile settled Molly, but it masked her own fears that her big day would be lucky if it went without a hitch. Secretly she was relieved to know that Molly had asked the doctor and his wife to come to the wedding, just in case he was needed. Dinah's face suddenly lit up to see the first cart to arrive.

"Here's Mum and she's laden with food, I'm so glad that she's come. Nellie's family are close by if she starts with the baby, as our Jim won't be much of a help at all."

Molly too peered through the window.

"Now it's William's carriage pulling up, and doesn't Emily look lovely?"

Dinah agreed and she could hardly wait for her to bring Molly's outfit up. They could hear the excitement as William greeted his brothers and the Bradmans were helping Peg to set the table downstairs.

Emily knocked on the bedroom door, her face beaming as she entered to see them. "Dinah, you are a most beautiful bride and that dress shows off your lovely figure, it could have been made for you. Hello, Molly, my you do look well."

195

"I'm well enough and very big thank you, but you look lovely Emily where did you get that outfit?"

"Thank you Molly, only it is a long story, but I do hope you will not be offended, because here is one for you."

She presented her parcel to Molly who on opening it gasped with delight.

"Is this really for me Emily, thank you so much, now how much do I owe you for it?"

"It is a gift from Ruth, Martha and I; we have gone into business making them." She then explained how it all worked along with the help of some ladies from the church.

"You are a clever girl!" Molly gasped. "I wondered how you'd manage for an income after giving up the school. Why didn't you tell me Dinah, when you came back that day?"

"It was my fault Molly as I swore them both to secrecy; because we wanted to make one for you as a surprise, please do not be angry with her."

"I could never be angry with her, not after she has worked so hard to make something to fit me for today. Now will please show me how this outfit works Emily?"

While the change of clothes was taking place, Harry's cart pulled up and Maggie began carrying some of the food in, leaving him to bring in his Elderberry wine. Tom helped a weary Alice from the cart, before settling her down in a comfortable chair. He then returned to the carry in the wedding cake for Maggie who was already taking in the remaining baking, he then went upstairs to join his brothers.

The Bradmans helped Maggie and Peg to fill the table, with a mouth watering display of food and lashings of fresh milk that Peg had brought. In the centre was Maggie's wedding cake taking pride of place as usual. While Harry then opened one bottle of his Elderberry wine, thinking that it would just start the celebrations off nicely. He handed it round to anyone who cared to partake of it with him. Unfortunately Maggie, Peg and the Bradmans were far too busy to bother.

Alice declined as she was exhausted, but didn't want to admit it. With all the men being upstairs there was more for Harry to enjoy by himself. Peg was eager to know how Alice was feeling after her long journey.

"You're looking well Alice; it's not much longer now, eh?"

"I'd like to see my feet again, but I'm well thanks Peg and how's Nellie?"

"She's as far gone as you and her family live down the lane so they'll see to her today."

"With so many of you ladies having babies," Martha said. "Lancashire will be swamped with Cardell offspring's for generations."

"I suppose you're right Martha, because in less than two years our family name will have doubled, who can say how many there'll be in ten years time."

"What a thought," Ruth joked. "That maybe hundreds of redheaded Cardells might end up owning most of the land around here."

"You're joking Ruth," Alice said. "I don't think I'll be having that many."

"You'll only need to have four each," Harry said. "That'll be sixteen, and if they all have four, you'll have your own dynasty in no time."

"Oh Harry!" Maggie gasped. "Have you been at the Elderberry wine already?"

Everybody laughed just as the brothers came down in time to catch Harry's prophecy. Tom did not comment, but left it to Bob as the groom to add his own views.

"Nay I think Dinah and me ought to get wed first dinna yee, but the idea of us having four bairns each, might be a bit on the short side Harry. Our parents had ten but three of them died, but if we've got our father's blood in our veins, then our dynasty will fill Lancashire in less than ten years."

The room erupted in laughter once again and he thought that this wedding day was one to be remembered for a long time.

"Never mind how many bairns yee might have," Dick said. "If we dinna get to the Kirk soon, yee'll have none."

They soon left in Dick and Molly's cart after Bob had helped him up. Harry, Maggie, Tom and Alice followed them. William, Emily and the Bradmans were hot on their heels. Later Peg proudly led Dinah out in her beautiful and elegant wedding dress, before helping her to sit up at the front next to her.

She then assisted Molly into the back who was wearing her smart new brown outfit. Peg was now excited about giving her daughter away and she drove very slowly all the way and many villagers smiled and the shopkeepers waved.

"I do hope everything goes all right Mum. I've a bad feeling something will spoil it."

"What, could possibly happen to spoil it for you?"

Dinah didn't want to tempt providence and say what exactly was worrying her, though the bright spring sun shone down as if to give her its blessing.

Outside the church Dinah's heart beat wildly with excitement mixed with trepidation, and she crossed her fingers just in case. She did not notice all the other carts already there, as Peg helped her and Molly down, leaving the cart ready for their return.

"Well, Molly, what do you think about your outfit now?" Dinah enquired.

"It was a lovely surprise, and you and Bob already knew didn't you?"

Dinah winked knowingly, before taking a deep breath as her mother took her arm ready to walk down the aisle.

"Are you ready Molly?" She enquired with a backward glance.

"As I'll ever be Dinah, but the size I am might block out the sunlight in the church."

Dinah giggled, and in her silk gown she glided through the church doors.

As she passed Maggie and Harry's family she smiled, but when Molly passed.

"My goodness!" Maggie gasped. "Our Alice hasn't put as much weight on as Molly has; I'm afraid she'll burst."

"Shush!" Harry warned. "She might hear you."

Tom and Alice had heard and he put his arm around Alice's ample frame to comfort her.

They were all seated on the front pew because Tom was the eldest brother. While William, Emily and the Bradmans sat behind them. Tom wondered how Dick would manage to walk up the aisle even though it was only a few months since he looked like he was at death's door, and he also wondered if Bob would be as nervous as he had been.

<u>Chapter 17 Bob`s wedding</u>

Earlier outside the church before the family came, Bob had helped Dick down from the cart and gave him his stick, before moving it away to make room for the others to come.

On entering church he checked.

"Yee've got the ring Dick, haven't yee?"

"Aye, it's safe in my pocket." He patted his britches.

Bob then noticed many farmers and their families had arrived and also many villagers all came to support them.

"It's a wee bit different from Tom and Alice's wedding." Bob muttered.

"Aye, but everyone's coming that's been asked."

"I'm glad Molly invited the doctor, Dinah was worried with Alice being near her time?" "Aye that's why she asked him, she too was worried."

"And poor Dinah's been too scared to say anything."

They waited for Tom and William's families to arrive.

"I'm glad the doctor and his wife are sitting on Dinah's side."

Everyone was there as the minister came out, so he and Dick stood up at the altar rails as the organ began. Nervous excitement ran through his body realising that Peg and Dinah were coming down the aisle with a heavily pregnant Molly following them.

There were oohs and arhs as she passed, Bob turned and she took his breath away. She looked a vision in her white tightly fitted gown, and in her long blonde hair were the spring flowers they had earlier picked. She made his heart race and her smile made him go weak at the knees, on reaching him the music stopped and the service began. Everything went to plan until the minister enquired.

"Does any person here, know of any reason why these two people may not be joined in holy Matrimony, speak now or forever hold your peace?"

There was the normal few moments' silence, which was suddenly perforated with a loud scream from Alice, who rolled over in pain clutching her stomach. Chaos erupted, Tom panicked and Maggie and Harry tried to calm her. Doctor Ward sprang from his seat and got her to the back of the church, so that the ceremony could continue. Tears ran down Dinah's face, as the congregation buzzed. Dick grabbed her before she fainted and Molly consoled her.

"Don't worry Dinah; I thought something like this might happen thank goodness I asked the doctor and his wife to come."

"Oh Molly," She sobbed. "And I was afraid to say anything."

"Never mind Dinah, it was only going to be the four of us anyway. Besides William, Emily, the Bradmans and Peg are still here and those at the back of the Kirk."

The disturbance eventually subsided, after everyone concerned had left for the mill.

"I'm sorry Reverend," Dinah said. "Please would you mind carrying on?"

The minister who was not accustomed to having his services disrupted nodded.

"If you are both ready, then we will proceed."

Dick held her hand until the minister concluded.

"I now pronounce that you are man and wife, you may kiss the bride."

At that he did, and the congregation clapped loudly, and as the organ struck up he proudly walked his new wife down the aisle.

"Ye look beautiful," He whispered. "And I love yee."

"I love you too, but I knew that something would spoil it."

"Nay nothing's spoilt it, or stopped us getting wed has it?"

"No, but all that fuss during the service."

"Nay I think yon Alice will be more distressed than yee."

"I'm sorry, but I wish I'd not made her come now."

"Dinah lassie, she risked everything to be at our wedding, just yee remember that."

Emily reached her before Peg; much to the latter's displeasure.

"You look radiant Dinah, much prettier than I did in that dress."

"Thanks Emily, but I don't feel very radiant, just look at my face. I think Agnes's curse has passed on to me, spoiling my wedding."

"Do not say that, we both got married in that dress, and poor Agnes did not. Besides I can only see a beautiful bride on the arm of her husband who loves her."

"I'm sorry for being so selfish Emily, now tell me how is Alice?"

"The doctor is with her, but at eight months it is a bad time for a baby."

Peg then pushed her way forward.

"Come on you two, so we can get you back to the mill."

"Yee take Dinah, as Dick and Molly canna drive their cart."

"Oh Bob!" she gasped. "Can't we go back together?"

"Aye, if Peg takes Dick and Molly back and we'll go in their cart if yee like?"

"Whatever!" Peg blustered. "As long as we all get back to the mill."

It was agreed, but Dick`s cart was blocked in, so he helped Dick and Molly into Peg's cart before returning. The congregation was beginning to come out and they all shook their hands as they waited. Eventually Bob brought the cart up.

"Let me help yee Mrs Cardell, in that lovely wedding dress?"

"Do you like it Bob? She blushed. "Wasn't it kind of Emily to lend it to me."

"Aye there's nere been a bonnier bride than yee Dinah lassie."

"Oh I wish we could go somewhere instead of the mill, there'll be an upset with Alice."

"The doctor is there, all thanks to Molly inviting him."

"I'm glad he came, but what did Emily mean that having a baby at eight months is bad?"

"I dinna ken but we'll soon find out, they'll all be there by now."

They reached the mill and all the carts and buggies were lined up outside.

"Look!" Dinah gasped. "William and Dick are by the mill and Tom's pacing about."

"I'll leave the cart here, while yee go and see what's happening with Alice, I've to see why Tom looks so grey poor thing."

"Can't we go in together Bob; I'm frightened that something's wrong."

"Come on then and I'll talk to him later, but yon looks in a bad state."

"He`s! In a bad state. "Dinah gasped. "And just how do you think poor Alice feels?"

It was quite clear that childbirth divided the sexes; even inside the house the women were the same. Harry sat by himself seeking solace in his Elderberry wine.

Peg and Mrs Ward were convincing Ruth and Martha to eat something, as they burst in.

"What's happening with Alice?" Dinah frantically asked.

"The baby's the wrong way round," Ruth explained. "And the doctor's trying to turn it." "Poor Tom's heartbroken," Martha said. "He thinks she and the baby will die."

"I'm away to see him Dinah, I'm sorry lassie but we men are nay as strong as yee are where bairns are concerned."

"Oh go then, and leave it to us. Dinah huffed. "Why aren't you with Alice, Mother?"

"Someone's to greet the bride, besides there's enough of them up there as it is."

"Molly and Emily are carrying babies; I can understand Maggie being there for her."

"Don't tell me you're going up in your wedding dress Dinah."

"I certainly am Mother."

She ran up the stairs picking up her gown only to hear Alice's screams coming from the small bedroom, and then she saw Emily and Molly pacing the floor in another bedroom. "What's happening is Alice going to be all right?"

"We don't know Maggie's in with the doctor so there's no room for us. We are waiting here in case they need boiling water or anything." Molly explained.

"You two should take care of the babies you're carrying. Now go down and rest then get my Mother to boil some water, and I'll stay here if they need me?"

"But, what about your dress Dinah, you might spoil it." Emily added.

"I'll get changed and you can take it back Emily and thanks for lending it to me."

"I am not concerned about that, if they do need you it will get in the way."

They reluctantly left and Dinah changed and removed the flowers from her hair before going in to see Alice.

Maggie was unsuccessfully trying to calm her down and made it harder for the doctor.

"Harry needs you Maggie." She suggested. "He's been at the Elderberry wine."

"But our Alice needs me more." Maggie argued.

"I'll stay with her; you'd better go and sober him up."

"Our Alice will be all right, won't she, doctor?"

"Yes," He assured her. "Go Maggie you've been a big help, but Dinah is here now."

She too reluctantly left.

"Right Dinah, calm Alice down, I know she's frightened but it's not helping."

"What are you going to do doctor?"

"I am going to turn the baby, but she has to keep very still."

"I'm here Alice, and it's going to be all right, now just take deep breaths in and out. That's right; now grasp my hand so the doctor can turn the baby."

"But it's not time yet, am I going to lose it?" Alice screamed.

Sweat poured off her worried brow so Dinah stroked her forehead and sang a soothing melody. "The flowers are blooming nigh and birds are flying high…"

It worked, as Alice's pulse rate then slowed down and her breathing returned to normal.

"That is good Alice; now take a deep breath while I turn the baby: it will be painful but it will not take long, are you ready?"

"I'll try doctor; oh will you hold me tight Dinah?"

She stopped Alice from seeing what was happening; singing again and holding her tight.

The doctor nodded and then began. Alice shrieked with pain and Dinah held her even tighter, stroking her brow all the time.

"There it is all done, and the baby is back where it should be, well done Alice."

Tears of relief ran down her face and Dinah wiped them away.

"What now doctor?" She whispered as Alice lay exhausted on the bed.

"She must rest for as long as possible, to let the baby settle."

"What if it doesn't?"

"Then the baby will be born a month early."

"Will it be all right?"

"It will have everything it needs but it will be small. The last month a baby puts on weight to give it a better chance for the birth."

"But they live at Blackmoor Moss and they're only here for the wedding."

"She had better not travel for a few days just to let things improve."

"Do have something to eat doctor?" Dinah said. "Remember you are still our guest."

"I could do with it, but Alice must rest, so I will ask her mother to come up."

"No, not yet doctor but please ask Molly to come instead, I've to talk to her?"

"I will tell Maggie what has happened, but who will tell Alice's husband?"

"When I've spoken to her, I'll tell Tom, and she'll stay with Alice."

"You have been very good Dinah, things got out of hand with Maggie."

"That's because Alice is her daughter, but she is my sister in law now."

"You have certainly proved yourself again and I am so glad that you were here?"

"Thanks doctor, but I didn't expect to spend my wedding day as a nurse."

"I think you should consider being one, the way you have coped with things?"

"I couldn't look after strangers, only for the people I love."

He nodded and left, it was then that she began to tremble just as Molly came in.

"Are you all right Dinah, you look dreadful?"

"I was so scared, but I put on a brave face."

"What a wedding day Dinah, now go and put your dress back on and the flowers in your hair and then go down? Maggie's itching to get back here, and has hidden the Elderberry wine from Harry. I've just seen Peg pouring herbal tea by the pot full down his throat."

"I'll put my flowers in water for Alice, she's earned them."

"What a lovely idea Dinah."

She then explained what the doctor said.

"If she can't travel yet, what shall we do?"

"Then she must stay here, but we can't put all of them up."

"They've to be back for milking, will you stay with Alice and I'll go and speak to Tom?"

"Of course, but don't forget it's still your wedding day."

"I'll change right now and I won't be long."

Downstairs she faced a barrage of questions from everyone, and excusing herself she went in search of Tom to tell him that Alice was all right, but she was totally unprepared for what awaited her.

207

Bob had earlier rushed out to see his brothers who appeared to be in shock.

"What's the matter with yee all?"

"It's Tom;" Dick explained. "None of us ken what he'd suffered all these years."

"What do yee mean?" Bob asked.

He saw his sombre looking eldest brother.

"Come on Tom, we ken yee're worried: but Alice is in good hands."

"What's the doctor say, Bob?" Tom grunted.

"The baby's the wrong way round…."

"I ken it;" Tom interrupted. "She and the baby are going to die, just like mother did?" "Mother, dinna have a doctor to help her, did she?" Bob argued.

"Nay, Bob yee're right, but hers was the wrong way too and look what happened then."

"We've tried to tell him things are different here," Dick explained. "Doctor Ward saved my life after that fall, if it had happened on the croft I'd have died for sure."

"It's like he's nay listening to us," William said. "His mind is in a mess."

"A mess" Bob asked. "What about William?"

"There's nay need to talk as if I'm nay here," Tom said. "Everything is my fault?" "What's all your fault?" Bob asked getting annoyed.

William and Dick sat on the mill steps and let him explain it all again to him.

"When Mother was having that bairn, I told Jinni I hoped it'd be the last. The croft was too wee, we five slept top to tail as it was. I said I hoped it was a lassie they had room."

"Yee are nay to blame for that Tom?" Bob said.

208

"Canna I Bob? I'd heard yon giving birth many times afore: only this time it was nay the same and I covered my head so as nay to hear her."

"Tom, yee were twelve years old," Bob comforted him. "What could yee have done?"

"William and I said that," Dick admitted. "But it dinna make any difference."

"Go on Tom," Bob urged. "Now you mun tell me the rest?"

"I could nay stand it and went in and Mother's face was pale with sweat. I begged Father to help her, but he just sat there.

I asked him what was wrong and he said the bairns coming feet first. I screamed at him to put it right and he yelled that if he could he would. Mother then stopped breathing and I shook her to bring her back."

His brothers felt sorry for him as he continued.

"I screamed again to get the bairn out and he pulled out a little lassie that was already dead. I put her in Mother's arms and cried. Father blamed me for them running away to the hills as their families dinna get on. They fell in love tending the goats and dinna ken which family they came from. They took a goat from each of their herds and ran as far as they could up into the highlands; but I dinna ken what that meant. I cleaned up the blood and made her and the bairn look like they were asleep, afore waking Jinni."

"I remember yee waking us up," Dick said. "Dinna yee Bob?"

"Aye and John could nay breathe when he carried yee in William."

"Nay I only ken yee all were crying, Jinni held Ellen and cried too."

"Yee still canna blame yee self, it might have been early like Alice." Bob explained

209

"Aye it's my punishment for blaming Father for nay saving her, now I ken how he felt?"

"Yee are wrong Tom," Bob replied. "Alice and yon bairn will nay die Doctor Ward`s there."

"I should nay have got Alice with child afore we wed, so now I'm paying for it."

"Nay Emily will tell yee of God's love and forgiveness, we nere ken about Him."

"I still dinna ken about God, appen that's what's wrong with me."

"Yee were a father to us Tom," Dick added. "So dinna be so hard on yeerself."

"It was only out of guilt Bob; and none of yee kens the truth."

"Yee canna have changed what happened," Bob insisted. "All yon years ago."

"I dinna ken, but it's happening now so I nay deserve to be happy." He sobbed bitterly before continuing to explain much more.

"Aye but when Maggie said our bairn would be spared the shame of nay having my name, that's when Father's words made sense to me."

His brothers listened in amazement.

"Aye we are all shamed by nay having our Father's name; we are all really Mc Kenzies."

There was a stunned silence until Dick reacted.

"Did yee ken this afore Molly and I wed?"

"Aye but only a week afore Dick and I ken yee'd told the minister yee name."

"Yee dinna tell me afore we got wed today, did yee?" Bob said angrily.

"It was nay good as we've been Cardells all our life and in our new lives too we have. How do yon think Peg, Maggie, Harry, and Reverend Parker would feel if they ken we were all shamed by nay having our Father's name, and wanted to wed their lassies?"

"It dinna make any difference to me and Emily getting wed, none of yee ken about that, so I canna see what good it would do if yee all had known."

"Yee're right as always William," Dick agreed. "So if we had nay ever met again then we'd nay have ken about it, would we?"

"Aye but if I'd ken about it and changed my name," Bob said. "It would be nay good for all of yee?"

Tom sighed with relief at last.

"Aye we'll all have to live with this." Bob suggested. "Our Toms carried this guilt all these years.

We should forget our parent's problems they did the best they could for us all, and Lord knows they had some sadness in their lives? Look! Here comes my beautiful bride?" He ran and kissed her, almost afraid to ask her how Alice was.

"I'm glad to see yee bonnie lassie, and yee'll nay believe what's happened."

"And you'll never believe what I've to tell you Bob; or Tom really."

"Nay dinna say its bad news, because he's expecting it to be?"

"Then he's going to be very disappointed, isn't he?"

"Aye then is everything all right?"

Her smile told him that it was, and they went over to tell an anguished Tom the news. "Come with us Tom, Doctor Ward's turned yon bairn and now Alice is resting."

The joy returned to his face as he dared to ask. "How's Alice and the bairn?"

Dinah repeated everything and then added.

"But she's to stay where she is for a while."

"Nay, but we must be away home." Tom frowned.

"I said I'd repay yee one day for letting me stay after yon wedding Tom." Dick reminded him.

211

"But yee've nay room for us all to stay Dick, have yee?"

"Yee and yon wife can stay, and we'll sort everything out later."

Tom smiled for the first time since leaving the church.

"Thanks Dick and all of yee for listening to my ranting."

Bob then spoke up for all of them.

"Tom we'll always be here for yee, even if yee have upset our wedding day."

"Sorry Bob, but I'm glad that yee're all there for me, I feel better now that yee all ken the truth at last."

"Aye and the truth is, some things in life are meant to be." Bob replied. "So it's nay use blaming yeerself anymore for any of it, Tom."

Bob and Dinah walked to the mill hand in hand in their wedding clothes and wondered what else life had in store for them. Tom followed them still in shock.

Later Dick and Molly talked things over with Bob and Dinah and eventually they came up with a solution which they put to Alice's parents.

"How yee feel Maggie and Harry if me and Dinah come back with yee today? It'll be our honeymoon and we'll help yee around the farm until Tom and Alice return."

Maggie was cheered about it after worrying about Alice.

"It would be lovely having you, but we wouldn't expect you to work, would we Harry?"

"You might not," He winked. "I'll have Bob up at the crack of dawn doing the milking."

The four laughed as they set out to Blackmoor Moss and Maggie talked all the way.

"You can spend your honeymoon in Tom and Alice's bedroom just like they did."

At the mill Tom and Alice had Bob and Dinah's room and he talked to his brother. "Thanks Dick and yee too Molly for letting us stay, I'll help yee in the mill or in anyway I can, I hope its nay too much for yee Molly having Alice here?"

"I'm not up to doing much Tom, but its nice having another sister around the place."

Alice's condition improved and the doctor gave his consent for her go home on Sunday.

At around dinner time Harry's cart pulled up and Maggie again was laden with food, Bob and Dinah looked glowing and happy in the back. They had only just joyfully greeted each other when Peg's cart drew up outside as it usually did on that day.

Dinah met her with a smiling face.

"You're just in time to share our meal Mum."

But Peg could not contain her excitement.

"I've come to tell you that I'm a granny."

"Well done Peg," Maggie said. "You've beaten me, but it won't be long for me too?"

"Thanks for making me into an aunty, a week after my wedding." Dinah joked.

"Are they both well?" Molly asked. "What did they have and what have they called it?"

"His name is James after my late husband and of course our Jim."

Bob felt sick at the thought of Jim glorifying in Fatherhood, when he had to wed Nellie. They all enjoyed Maggie's spread and chatted easily till Harry soon suggested.

"We'd best make a move to get our Alice back home before she does have this baby."

Bob and Dinah thanked Harry and Maggie for having them; likewise in their turn they thanked them both for helping on the farm. Before they left Tom and

Alice thanked Dick and Molly for letting them stay, and apologised for spoiling Bob and Dinah's wedding.

"Aye and I'm only too glad to repay yee for yon kindness in letting me stay with yee."

"That goes for me too; take care Alice and let us know when the baby comes; I'll not be much longer myself having these twins."

The four of them smiled as they waved off, Harry and family on their way to Blackmoor Moss. Tom smiled cuddling Alice wondering what he and his brothers' bairns would all be, and there was still time yet for Bob and Dinah to have one in this year of 1747.

Chapter 18 back on Skye

It was June 1746 on Skye and sixteen year old Ellen's curly red hair shone in the sun, as she returned with peat for the winter fire.

"I've left it outside yon shelter for John to stack after he's milked the goat."

Twenty three year old Jinni flicked her long auburn hair out of her eyes and smiled. "Thanks love, but why do yee look sad again?"

"Nay I've given up looking now, I dinna ken they'll ere come back."

"We canna nay believe it Ellen." Jinni said. "John would nay live if he thought that."

"Aye at least he is helping us now, but it's hard for him in the winter."

The croft door opened and John carried the milk pail in.

"I've stacked the peat Ellen and yon goats are nay happy sharing their shelter."

His blonde hair now bleached with the sun and his blue eyes glinted.

"Aye thanks John; do yee remember a goat kicking Thomas so hard it twisted his tooth?"

"Dinna they throw stones up to see which of them had to milk it?"

"Nay did they really do that, John?" Ellen asked.

"Aye and I was glad that Thomas dinna let me do it then."

"Oh John yee look just like Mother today." Jinni said.

"Thanks Jinni, it's a pity I dinna look and feel as well in winter though."

"Did yee bring any stones back, Ellen?"

"Aye but yee canna still be putting them on their graves, are yee Jinni?"

"There's nay chance I'll have any bairns, like Mother did," She bit her lip. "We dinna have a soul coming by here, not since the Laird's men, that is. Anyway I'm away to the burn for water, yee two keep that pot boiling and I'll make some broth when I fetch some herbs and wild garlic on the way back."

Ellen and John nodded as she left.

Jinni's arms were full carrying everything back, when she noticed four horsemen thundering towards her and her heart leapt.

"Aye they're home at last!" She muttered excitedly to herself but her joy soon turned to fear as one of the strangers dismounted.

"Aye I'm sorry to scare yee lassie, but could yee spare a drink, we've travelled hard?"

She felt vulnerable even though she wasn't far from the croft.

"Nay I've only got this pail, but yee can have that."

"Thank yee kindly lassie." He smiled.

She watched this attractive young man hand it to a man on one of the horses and heard him call him sire.

"Aye and whose yon man yee're calling sire, and why should he drink first?"

"This is Charles Edward Stuart; and it is our honour as loyal Mc Donald kinsmen, to see the Prince safely to his ship that will take him back to France."

"Aye and it's his fault that my brothers were taken away to fight for him."

"Nay lassie yon is the true the King of England and Scotland."

"King of wherever!" She ranted. "Why is he safe and my brothers are still missing?"

"Aye but his army was killed at Culloden."

"Killed, all of them?" Jinni screamed." How did yee escaped and my brothers' dinna?"

"We only escaped with the help of our kinswoman Flora Mc Donald; she crossed the water and disguised us all as serving lassies. Aye but many deserted before that."

Jinni wept and young man comforted her, as the others watched with compassion.

"What's yee name lassie? I'm Alex Mc Donald and the younger laddie at the back is my wee brother Malcolm, we are Flora McDonald's kinsmen, and yon other fiercer looking one is a friend called Rob McLeish."

"I'm Jinni," She sobbed. "Jinni Mc Cardell."

As Alex comforted her, she noticed him look at his brother and then removed his arm.

"Aye and we'll call on our way back, to help yee Jinni."

The other two men nodded as he remounted, then the Prince looked at her with pity in his eyes, before they all left in a cloud of dust. Jinni watched them leave before refilling the pail, unsure if she should tell John and Ellen when she retuned to the croft.

"Aye are yee all right Jinni?" Ellen asked. "Have yee been crying?"

"Nay it's the wild onions I picked they got in my eyes," She lied. "And I found mushrooms to go with herbs for our soup tonight."

For three days, Jinni hid the news from them, but on the fourth her heart chilled, as the three of them returned. John was milking at the back and Ellen was out collecting peat. Jinni could not understand why it pleased her to see Alex again, as he went in the croft.

"I have nay been honest with yee Alex; I live with my brother John, who has a bad chest, and a younger sister Ellen, who is out at the moment."

217

"Dinna worry, what we can do, to make up for yon missing brothers?"

"Aye well yon roof needs changing afore winter as the fire makes it so damp."

"We'll do that, but dinna the damp upset yon brother's chest?"

"Aye it might, but we canna do without the fire to cook on and to keep us warm."

"Where's yon straw?" Rob asked removing his dirk from its sheath: as did the other two.

Jinni took them round to the shelter, where John was finishing the milking and he looked shocked to see her with the men.

"John, these men called a few days ago, they fought with our brothers and they're going to replace the straw on the roof, it's hard for us to do isna it?"

"Nay why should they? John asked. "And why are yon safe and where are our brothers?"

"Aye we'll tell yee now John, or will yee wait till Ellen comes back?"

"Aye I think yee better had, we dinna have folks come to our home."

"I'll make us all a drink until Ellen returns, she'll nay be long."

They all trooped into the croft and it was then that Alex mentioned.

"Jinni tells me yee suffer with yon chest in the winter, John?"

"Aye and it's been like it all my life."

"So why do yee think it's worse in the winter?" Alex asked.

"I canna go out then, as the winds take my breath away."

"So do yee mean; yee are always indoors with yon fire going?"

"Aye, we have the fire or we'd freeze to death."

218

"If yon smoke canna escape, that'll make yee chest worse."

' "There's nay anything we can do about that, is there?"

John was angry and gasped for breath, which proved Alex's point.

In the midst of this heated debate Ellen returned, not surprised to see three strangers, as their horses were outside, and she was angry at the row that was going on.

"Aye and why's John upset, and just who and why are yee here?"

"Ellen, this is Alex Mc Donald, his brother Malcolm, and their friend Rob McLeish, and they all fought with our brothers."

"So why canna they be with yee?" She asked.

"Nay we were on horseback," Alex said. "And that's how we got away from Culloden."

"Aye, so what's a Culloden?" Ellen asked.

"Culloden is a field, where the Jacobite army were killed."

"What! All of them except yee three?" Ellen's eyes filled with tears.

"Aye those who reached Culloden did, but like I told Jinni, many deserted afore that."

"So, they may still be alive somewhere, is that what yee're saying?"

"Aye Ellen, that's what I'm saying."

"And do yee think they'll nay come back, Alex?"

Malcolm came to his brother's aid, to try and calm down this feisty young woman.

"Do yee think Ellen, there's much to offer them to come back for?"

"I've been hanging on for them." John shrieked. "Yon lassie can nay live here, if I die."

"Oh John, don't say anything about dying." Jinni begged. "We canna lose yee too."

She wept so Alex put his arm around her again, and Ellen was shocked to see it.

Rob tried to ease things.

"Aye and another winter here will only make John's chest worse, why dinna yee all come down to the lowlands with us? The sea air is grand and with some proper treatment, it'll make a big difference to him."

Ellen looked to Jinni, while John was sceptical and asked.

"Aye but what if our brothers come home, how will they ken where we are?"

"We could leave them a note, on yon door." Rob suggested.

"That's nay good we canna read." Ellen explained.

"Aye well it's up to all of yee; we've three horses that can take yee down." Rob said.

Jinni as the mother figure took control.

"He's right, they canna come back, there was nay enough to feed us all, when they left. "But its John that matters now, what do yee both think?"

"Aye and it's me making yee do this, do yee all want to go?" Alex asked.

"John" Jinni said. "We'll be together, isna that right, Alex?"

"Aye but yee lassies will be at our Mother's, John will stay at Rob's a few doors away, and it's his Mother and sister Aisla work wonders with herbs and things."

"Aye, but we canna leave yon goats behind." John asked.

"Then we'll take them with us; we've twine to keep them close." Alex said.

"It looks like we're away then, we'll wrap John up to keep him warm." Ellen said.

She remembered how he had looked after her and William, when they were young.

Outside Rob secured the goats to Alex and Malcolm's saddles, while the brothers helped John onto his horse, it being the biggest.

Inside, Jinni and Ellen tipped the water onto the fire, and for the first time in their lives, they saw it go out. They looked around the croft for the last time, remembering the happy and sad times they had spent there, before shutting the door on their old lives.

Malcolm helped Ellen up to sit in front of him, while Alex did the same for Jinni, who looked back at the hillside where the family's graves were. She had never expected that their lives were to change so fast, and to begin a new one with a future that could be better for all of them, especially for John. They travelled the same way their brothers did.

"What were yon parents called Jinni?" Alex asked.

"Father was Tommy and Mother was Jennet, why do yee ask?"

"Yon father was of the Mc Cardell clan and yon mother was of the Mc Kenzie clan, and they both came from the lowlands?"

"Nay our parents have always lived here, yee are wrong."

"Mother told us that about twenty six years ago, Tommy Mc Cardell met Jennet Mc Kenzie and they fell in love. They ran away to the highlands, the rumours were she was with child and their families would have killed them if it was true."

"Did yee say, twenty six years ago?"

"I ken it was nay yee Jinni, yee're too young."

"Aye but my brother Thomas is older, does this mean, that we're all Mc Kenzies? It's a good job he'll nay ken about it that's all I can say."

221

"That's what worried me and Malcolm, when yee told us yon name, so we think yee'd best say yee're all Mc Donald kinsfolk. So that neither of the clans will cause yee any harm, what do yee think?"

"Aye but we'd best tell the others about this, afore we get there."

"Malcolm and Rob are telling them; we'd talked about it afore we came back to yee."

"Aye well if yee ken all about this, then why did yee come back at all?"

"Why do yee think Jinni?" He squeezed her tightly.

His words sent a thrill down her spine that she never felt before, making her blush.

"Aye but what's it like in the lowlands, I've nay heard of it afore?"

"Did yee ken that yee live on an island, called Skye?"

"What's an island, the only sky I ken is above my head?"

"An island is land surrounded by water, people down yonder fish for their livelihood, they get weeds from the sea called sanforth which they boil and eat."

"Aye and will it be the same sea that Charles Stuart sailed away on?"

"Aye, but the sea turns into what they call an ocean."

"The only water I've ken is from the burn, but my brothers must have seen it after they were taken away from us."

"Aye they not only saw it, they were taken across it to Scotland."

"What's a Scotland?"

"Jinni dear, yee do have a lot to learn, I'll teach yee about England too."

"What's an England? Aye we did have a sheltered life dinna we?"

"I promise to always shelter yee Jinni."

"Dear Alex, I'll hold yee to that."

She was then so sure they had made the right decision to come with these men that they had not known very long. It was to be a new life and she hoped they were all up to it.

They eventually arrived in the lowlands and Mrs Mc Donald welcomed the sisters warmly and Mrs McLeish and her daughter Aisla did the same with John.

The girls listened intently eager to learn where they had originally come from.

"Yee lassies have the Mc Cardell look, but John, well he's is a true McKenzie."

"We ken John was like Mother, but we're all different shades of red."

"My sons were right to suggest yee say yee are McDonald kinsfolk, with that colour hair. Did yee say nobody came to yon house, till the Laird's men?"

"Aye a strange man once called, and he'd all sorts of odd things on his cart. I was only a wee bairn then, John, William and Ellen were nay even born, and Father was out in the fields with the Thomas, Richard and Robert."

"What happened then?" Mrs Mc Donald persisted.

"Mother gave him her pendant and he gave her a roll of plaid, needles and thread. Mother said I dinna have tell, but Father must have wondered where it came from. He used to carve wood into birds and animals, and he'd be away off somewhere and return with seed to sow and tools. I never ken where he went, and it was odd as he used to say that the less folk ken where we lived the better. He said if the Laird found out, he'd want rent off us. Nay one else came, why do yee ask Mrs Mc Donald?"

She listened and then began to explain everything that she knew.

"A tinker came many years back, trying to sell a pendant. One of the Mc Kenzie women bought it and wanted to ken where he got it from, but he said he'd been all over the highlands, so he dinna remember. There was a right to-do when it came to light, because old Mrs Mc Kenzies gave it to her daughter Jennet, years afore she disappeared, and she thought she was dead. Yet yee father carved wood as his brothers who had the same names as yon brothers all learnt it from their Father."

"I canna believe it, did nay one ever try to find mother?" Jinni asked and yet she and Ellen felt very afraid, but they waited with bated breath to hear Mrs Mc Donald tell the rest of the story.

"As yee ken Tommy Mc Cardell disappeared at the same time, it was afeared that he had killed Jennet, and fled in fear of his life in case the McKenzie clan did the same to him. But when the pendant was returned, the McKenzie's dinna give the Mc Cardells a chance to find out about it."

"Mrs Mc Donald, do we still have kin here from both families?" Ellen asked.

"Aye Ellen, but if either side found out about yee, the feuding would carry on. Now let's nay talk about it again, just be careful what yee say to anyone."

They took her advice and began their new lives; it was nice for a change for Jinni to be a young woman for the first time by allowing Mrs Mc Donald to mother her.

John's health improved too all thanks to the care and attention of Aisla and Rob's mother, combined with the smoke from the fire, escaping through a hole in the roof. In time he joined Alex, Malcolm and Rob on their fishing boats, enjoying life at sea.

Jinni and Ellen soon learnt how to gut and smoke the fish they caught, and how to get on with the lowland people, without giving themselves away. This was a completely new experience for all of them. They felt it was strange seeing faces and names that resembled their missing brothers, while others had their mother's fair hair and blue eyes, which made John, feel good about things.

Jinni and Ellen had many admires from the Mc Cardell clan, which upset Alex and Malcolm. While John had the McKenzie lassies in a spin about him, which also made Aisla jealous, because she had a soft spot for the now healthy and tanned young man. Life had changed irrevocably for the three siblings, though they never ever gave up hope, that their brothers would return safe and sound one day.

Epilogue

Tom, Alice, Maggie and Harry retuned home and as instructed contacted their own doctor. Alice had a long and protracted labour and two weeks later she gave birth to a son. They named him Thomas Henry Cardell as they had previously arranged much to Tom's and her parent's delight. The following June Molly went into labour early with the doctor and Dinah in attendance. She gave birth to a boy they called Samuel and a girl called Annie, named after her parents who owned the mill. Dick was overjoyed that both children had survived, unlike his own mother's twins. Emily and William's baby was born a week early; it was a boy that they named John, after the brother who cared for him after the death of their parents. Ruth and Martha were thrilled, but continued to help the ladies in the outhouse to make more maternity clothes. This allowed Emily to care for the baby. On Christmas day of the same year Dinah gave Bob the best present ever, a beautiful blue eyed blonde haired daughter just like his mother and brother John. They named her Ellen after his youngest sister. 1747 had indeed been a prolific year for the Cardell family because back on Skye Jinni, Ellen and John got married and each had produced children. Jinni married Alex and had a girl she named Jennet after her mother. Ellen married Malcolm had a boy she named Thomas after both her father and eldest brother. John whose health had improved married Aisla also became a father to a blonde blue eyed girl who he named Annie after his late twin sister who died at birth and that he had never met.